J F HOBB
Hobbs, Valerie.
Get it while it's hot--or
not : a novel /

D1566120

Get It While It's Hot.
Or Not.

A Richard Jackson Book

How Far Would You Have Gotten
If I Hadn't Called You Back?

Get It While It's Hot, Or Not.

a novel by

VALERIE HOBBS

Orchard Books   New York

Orchard Books, 95 Madison Avenue, New York, NY 10016

Book design by Mina Greenstein

Manufactured in the United States of America
The text of this book is set in 11 point Aldus Roman.
2   4   6   8   10   9   7   5   3   1

Library of Congress Cataloging-in-Publication Data
Hobbs, Valerie.
Get it while it's hot—or not : a novel / by Valerie Hobbs.
p.   cm.
"A Richard Jackson book"—Half t.p.
Summary: When she learns that her friend is pregnant,
Megan, a high school junior, begins to question
some of the promises she has made to others and to
herself.
ISBN 0-531-09540-1.   ISBN 0-531-08890-1 (lib. bdg.)
[1. Friendship—Fiction. 2. Youth—Sexual behavior—
Fiction.
3. High schools—Fiction. 4. Schools—Fiction.]   I. Title.
PZ7.H65237Ge   1996
[Fic]—dc20   96-15140

Get It While It's Hot.
Or Not.

What does it mean to be friends till the end? I thought I knew. I thought Kit knew, and Mia and Elaine. I thought we knew exactly what we were saying from the day back in eighth grade when we made our four banners. FRIENDS TILL THE END, we promised, and wrote the words on butcher paper in glue sprinkled with gold glitter. I guess we thought it would be easy, that all we'd have to do is say the words and write them, that we'd never have to think about what they really meant. We just felt so lucky to have found each other, we had to write it somewhere.

What began with a junior-high poetry project seems so long ago now, but my banner hangs over my dresser just like it did then, along with our eighth-grade graduation picture, the four of us arm in arm, all with goofy eighth-grade grins, three in braces, one looking like she'll blow away in a high wind. Friends till the end.

A year ago we got our first look at what "the end" might mean. Now the words we wrote so freely catch my eye each time I leave my room. They demand my attention. They make me think about the power words have and how people are changed by them. "A man's only as good as his word," Dad says. "Well, *people*," he corrects himself before I can needle him. "People are only as good as their word." All my life I've heard that, but now Kit's in trouble again and I'm hearing it in a different way.

Kit lives down the street from me in an old ramshackle Victorian built by her great-grandfather. It's all lace and gingerbread, three stories and a real attic, the most beautiful house in the city in its time. Now it's a "disgrace," according to my mother. And it really is pretty sad looking with its peeling paint and broken railings, its yard overgrown with weeds. "Like an old lady down on her luck" is the way Dad sees it.

Luck is something that went out the attic window with Kit's father about the time Kit was born. Actually he went out the front door, which Kit says she remembers vividly. I tell her she was too young to remember. "You'd be surprised what babies know," Kit declares, as if she's now an expert on the subject.

It's Tuesday morning, and Kit's curled up in an afghan on the couch. She's been crying. In my mother's words, the Clausens' living room looks like a cyclone's hit it, but that's normal for the Clausens. A worn braided rug is kicked off to one side, and the scuffed wooden floor is littered with newspapers and torn magazines. Every piece of furniture is stacked with something—clothes, magazines, dirty dishes, the cats, Minky and Squeak. A dying spider plant droops down the side of a bookcase. *General Hospital* is on the TV, one of those black-and-white things with the rabbit ears and perpetual snow.

"I have to go to bed," Kit says. Not even a hello.

"So . . .?" I lift Minky off the couch and sit in the warm spot he's left behind. He's a good cat, never holds a grudge. In two minutes he's up turning circles in my lap.

"You don't get it, Megan," she says. "In bed for the *rest of the time*. For the whole two months!"

When I ask why, Kit is her usual vague self. "Toxic something, I dunno. I'm a walking garbage dump."

"Kit!"

"*What?*" She pouts when you push her where she doesn't want to go.

"Toxemia is serious. The General says—" Kit usually listens when I quote my mother. She's head nurse in PEDS (short for pediatrics) and knows her stuff. I call her the General (never to her face of course), and so does Dad sometimes.

"It's too late to worry about it, Megan," Kit says, kicking off the afghan. "What I don't exactly need is somebody to help me worry!" In her sweats she doesn't look a whole lot different from her old self, a skinny, almost pretty girl with thin pale blond hair. In her sweats you can hardly tell she's pregnant, which is why we haven't talked a lot about it. Not since the rainy day when we'd gone to the Coffee Cat as usual after school, dying for a caffeine fix, soaked to the skin.

Before the miracle rain that day in October, our city had been in a drought for six years. The General, who volunteers on about nineteen different committees, was working overtime on Water Resources and Reclamation, getting ready to turn the ocean into drinking water. "And the drinking water into wine!" Dad said. "If anybody can do it, darling, you can."

The Cat was, as usual, jammed with kids. It's always

noisy, but the booths are private and nobody listens to what anybody says, anyway. Lots of secondary smoke danger, which Mia contributes to, but which we never thought much about until Kit told us about the baby.

"Promise you won't hate me," she began. No alarms went off since Kit says this all the time. It has to do with the level of her self-esteem, which we are constantly trying to hitch up a notch or two. We said all the right things, crossed our hearts. "Of course we won't hate you!" Kit can get pretty dramatic, but usually the big things she has to tell us fizzle out like foam on a cappuccino. This time she didn't waste any words. "I'm four months pregnant," she said.

That's all. Just that.

Kit has this weird way of going totally blank. I've seen her do it at school after she's raised her hand and then forgotten what she wanted to say, and I've seen her do it when her mother comes in drunk from work. Kit just freezes over, and you can't tell what she's thinking or if she's thinking at all.

I guess we froze, too. At least, that's what I remember. It was as if the collective wind had been knocked right out of us. Kit pregnant? How could that be? She was one of *us*. Rain pelted the windows. People walking past melted together in a stream of blue and green, yellow and red.

Mia got her breath back first. "You're kidding. *Kit!*" She leaned across the table and got right in Kit's face. Her whisper came out like an angry hiss. "You *can't* be pregnant."

Kit never blinked.

Elaine's eyes met mine. Hers were filled with tears on the verge of spilling. I curled my hand around Kit's. Her small hand was cold, clammy, as if she hadn't yet dried out from the rain. "Kit, what happened?"

"What do you think happened, dummy?" Mia shoots sparks in every direction when she's angry. She doesn't care where they land. I knew she wasn't angry at me or even at Kit, but I wasn't sure Kit knew. "It doesn't take a genius to figure this one out. Who's the lucky father, Kit?"

Kit blinked several times, then shook her head. She looked down at her hands. She has almost no fingernails, just the little bits she can't get to with her teeth. She shrugged. "I'm not sure," she said. Her pink-rimmed eyes looked rabbitlike and defensive.

"Oh, Kit, no. This is terrible." Elaine had gotten ahold of herself. Now she just looked horrified. It was hard not to put yourself in Kit's shoes, even if you'd never had sex, which was true for Elaine and almost true for me.

"I told you guys," Kit said in a monotone, as if she'd recorded ahead of time what she was going to say and then just pushed a button. "I told you that you'd hate me."

The rain came sideways, slapping the window in spiteful gusts. The door rattled as people blew in off the sidewalk. I began babbling, which I always do in times of crisis. "Nobody hates you, silly," I said. "We're just . . . surprised. I mean, you never said—about anyone—I mean, not since—not about *anyone*—"

"Much less *two*," Mia said, blowing smoke rings into the air that hung like permanent smog over our heads. She raised her dark eyebrows. "Three?"

Kit looked confused, but still she said nothing. I did it for her: "Knock it off, Mia."

"Okay, that's enough, you guys. *Hands!*" Elaine demanded, and put her own hand facedown in the middle of the table. In the way we always have, I put mine on top of hers. When Kit couldn't seem to move, I took hers and laid it on mine.

That left Mia. We all waited. Mia blew some more smoke. She laughed once, but her laugh had a hard edge to it. Then she just shook her head and sighed. "Well, I guess it could have been me, right?" she said with a grim smile. "Glass houses and all that!" She cupped Kit's hand with hers. Kit came slowly out of her fog, safe again at least for the moment, in that little world we made for ourselves in the booth at the Coffee Cat.

Minky farts. It isn't one of his most endearing traits. I shake him down off my lap. "So you have to hang out in bed for a while. That's not so awful. You can still finish school"—I pick cat hairs one by one off my lap—"if that's what you're worried about. You weren't intending to go right to the end anyway, were you?" Up till now, since Kit's so small, nobody's had to know.

"It's not that." Kit twirls a hunk of hair around her finger like spaghetti, letting it go and twirling it up again. "It's not school. I just don't want to be . . ." She looks around wide-eyed, up at the dusty molding hung with cobwebs, across the ceiling, and back again as if she's seeing it all for the first time. Her eyes are teary. "Here. Alone."

I bite back the urge to agree. Especially at night, it's the kind of house Hollywood producers pay big bucks to film slasher movies in. "Who says you're going to be alone? If the doctor says to stay in bed, that means somebody's got to be here with you. To get you things. You know, to cook and stuff."

I can see what Kit's thinking: to make sure I stay clean. Kit believes we pulled her through the last time, when drugs were her way to deal with troubles. Maybe we did. Maybe it was her shrink. Maybe it was prayer. Maybe it was just plain luck. But whatever it was, none of us ever wants to go through that again.

Finally I ask, because it's one of those things you have to ask, "What did your mom say?"

"She said I got myself into this mess—"

"And you have to get yourself out. Nice." Pretty much what I guessed.

"Well, you know Shirley."

A cute young doctor is doing a little open-heart surgery on *General Hospital*. In a snowstorm, or so it appears. "Well, I'll tell you one thing. You've got to have a better TV," I say. "Two months of this, and you'll go blind."

"Meg?"

"Yeah?"

"I lied."

I give Kit a sour look. *"Right!* You're not pregnant. You swallowed a volleyball."

"No, really. I lied about the father. I do know."

I check to see if she's putting me on. "You do?"

"You know I don't sleep around," Kit says with a little more life. "You know that, don't you?"

What did I know really? Anything? "Of course I do, silly."

Kit smiles slyly. "What would you say if I told you it was Monk?" Kit enjoys watching my jaw drop. Monk, captain of the basketball team, and Tiffany, Queen of

Everything, have been together since homecoming. Monk's taken. Monk is in another league. With his mean green Mustang and his zillion friends, Monk is definitely off-limits. "I'm growing one for the NBA," she says, patting her stomach.

"But *why*, Kit?"

"Why? For a million dollars, why else? Put Oprah on, will you?" I change the channel. Oprah, wearing her size seven jeans, sashays up the aisle, waving her microphone like a baton.

"You know what I mean, damn it. Why Monk? Why anybody? We said we weren't going to do it until we were at least eighteen, remember? What happened to that?"

Kit's face clouds over. She's lost somewhere far from me and this couch. "He said . . . You won't believe this." She looks up as if to make sure it's me and not somebody who won't try to understand. "He said he's had this crush on me for months but that he didn't want to hurt Tiffany. That's why we had to sneak around, he said. So she wouldn't get hurt. He was going to break up, let her down easy. Oh, Meg, why did I believe that? I feel like such a sleaze!"

Minky farts right on cue. "*He's* the sleaze," I tell her. "You're too trusting—that's all." Kit and Monk. Kit and *Monk*? It just won't compute. "Does he know?"

Kit pulls the afghan up and curls it around her face. "What good would it do to tell him?" she says miserably. "He'd just hate me."

"So? He's responsible, Kit. He's got to pay child support, at least that." At times like this, I wish Kit had a little Mia in her. Mia would fight, stand up for herself. Kit just rolls over like a possum and covers her eyes.

"Nobody's gonna know, Meg. Promise. Just you guys.

I don't want him near me. It just reminds me what a fool I've been."

I don't say anything for what seems like a long time, thoughts zinging through my head. At least I can tell Mia and Elaine. "Okay, I promise. But think about it, Kit. I mean, how are you going to take care of the baby? Your mom hardly makes it now." Shirley's Place, a bar on the lower west side, caters to lowlifes, and not enough of them to make a decent profit. What little she had saved went for Kit's therapy, which she's still paying off.

"We'll work it out," Kit says with a sudden spark of new confidence.

We? I set Minky on the floor and go into the kitchen, thinking Kit couldn't mean her and Shirley. Does she mean her and me? The four of us? Who else is there? Friends till the end, right? I think about all our plans for junior year, how it was going to be the best year yet, the most fun, our first real prom. So much for plans. With a sinking heart, I slap together a couple of PBJs and carry them into the living room on paper towels. Kit's staring at the TV, but I can tell she's not really watching it. Oprah looks straight into the camera. "You can lose it just like that," she says, and snaps her skinny fingers. I don't know what she's talking about, but I know she's right. She always is.

Reggie's Fat Burgers. Wednesday, lunch break. Elaine draws a perfect freehand time chart on a sheet of graph paper. "Okay," she says. "Mia, I know you aren't exactly Miss Early Bird, but you're the only one without a first period. I'm putting you down for seven. Seven until nine, the breakfast shift." Before Mia can protest, Elaine writes her name in bold black letters in four squares of the chart. "Mr. Armstrong lets me do pretty much whatever I want." She writes *Elaine* in two squares. "There, that gets Kit to lunch."

"Maybe I could cut History," I suggest. If any class should be cut, it's Worfley's American History. Worfley's History is the history of war, with a particular emphasis on the Korean Conflict, which he won single-handedly.

"Since when do you cut class?" Elaine says. "And don't say you'll quit the *Trib*, either. You're the only reporter who can write. I'm putting you down for after school." She writes my name in neat block letters. "And you can do dinner, right? At least on the days that the General's at the hospital. Mia can check in after work." She glances up at Mia, who we know is thinking about Mando. "Okay, okay, you can *call* from work. And if Kit needs you, then you go over."

Mia frowns. "What if Kit's mother's home?" Mia and Shirley don't get along. It's like shaking two snakes in a sack.

"Then you inquire, *politely*," Elaine says, "about the health of our friend and leave. Hey, we can do this!" She holds up her neatly drawn chart for everyone to admire. Mia looks doubtful, the way I feel. Charts worry me. They always make things look too easy.

For two of us, it will be easy, or if not easy at least doable. If Elaine's mother found out what we were planning, she'd probably start sending food over like care packages to flood victims. And Mia lives with her aunt Libby, who's only ten years older than she is and might as well be her sister. Mia, as she likes to remind us, runs her own life.

My case is different. I've been told in no uncertain

terms to stay away from the Clausens', that my reputation is in great danger. "She who lies down with dogs gets up with fleas," the General says. It's enough to make you itch. I stare at Elaine's chart, but in my mind I see the General bearing down, breathing fire. I consider being straight with her. I immediately reconsider. This is what it means to lie down with the dogs, she'd say. You get puppies.

I stuff everybody's fries in my mouth as we work out the last details. The fries are cold and don't taste like real potatoes. I heard somewhere they're making them out of plastic now, or out of soybeans or something. But that doesn't stop me from eating every last one. Maybe I'll do a story on it. "A moment on the lips . . . ," Mia reminds me, but I don't care. At least I'm not pregnant.

Looking back, it's easy to see the dreaded poetry project as one of the best things that could ever have happened in what looked to be a thoroughly rotten eighth-grade year. That was when the General decided that the house we had lived in since I was born would no longer "do." We would have to move. Not only was the house suddenly all wrong, the middle school was too. Things had changed at La Mesa since Danny, my brother, went there. Now there was a "bad element." Did I know there were gangs? Kids who wore their hats backward? All the good teachers were leaving. No one knew why things had changed, but no daughter of hers was going to a Second-Rate School. She started looking for houses the way she did everything else, which meant she'd find one in about half an hour.

When the General makes up her mind, it's a truly awesome thing. She lifts an eyebrow, daring you to challenge her, smug as a cat who's picked just the right bird down to its tiny bones. I cried and begged nonstop for a week, threatened to run away, promised to do the dishes every night for the rest of my life without uttering so much as a sigh. Even my brother, Danny, said Mom was wrong, but she just wouldn't listen. I pleaded with Dad. I'd die in the new school, I said. I wouldn't know a soul. For the first time in my life, I'd be "that new kid" (always weird).

My father, a lawyer, understood how hard it would be to leave old friends behind, his hand gripping my shoulder like I was a golf buddy who hadn't made the first-round cut. But my mother was right, he said. Lincoln was the better school. I'd be better prepared for Taylor High and A Good College, which was his goal in life for his children. I'd make new friends at Lincoln, he said, "the very best friends a girl could ever have." "Oh, Daddy," I cried in dramatic despair, "*you* don't know!"

But he did know, or else he just made a great guess. Ms. Whitcomb was my English teacher that year. I tried not to like her, just as I worked very hard at not liking anything at Lincoln. But Ms. Whitcomb was one of those people born to be liked. The General (who, to my everlasting embarrassment, makes it a point to meet all my teachers) said Sue Whitcomb was "charming and terribly bright," but it was more than that. She genuinely liked kids, all kids, even the ones who sat in the back row drawing marijuana leaves on their desks. And she was relentless, cheerfully relentless. After a while, even the worst kids gave up and got into whatever Ms. Whitcomb asked of them.

The poetry project would be fun, she said. (Several groans and rude comments from the back of the room.) We'd do our research with the library's brand-new CD-

ROMs. We'd "zip right down the information highway," the first fully computerized class in the county. We'd work in what she called "collaborative groups." To a new kid who knew hardly anybody, it all sounded terrifying.

She listed our names on the board in groups of four, mine first. Megan Lane, both names. No matter how you say it, and there's really only the one way, it sounds like the name of a street. Turn right on Laguna, go three blocks, then left on Megan Lane. My ears started to ring, which is what happens to this very day, whenever I get nervous. Who would I be stuck with? Who out there was already worried about being stuck with me? Megan Lane, the One Who Does Not Speak. Then in her flowing, elegant script, Ms. Whitcomb wrote *Elaine Capritto* and dotted both *i*'s.

Elaine was the girl with all the answers. She didn't even try to be cool, just stuck her hand in the air every time the teacher asked a question, her wide brown eyes sparkling with energy. "Yes, Elaine?" Ms. Whitcomb would say, and Elaine would spill out the answer. Always the right one, of course. I figured she'd be useful for the project. She probably read poetry, which, for most of us, was some particularly medieval form of torture. Under Elaine's name Ms. Whitcomb wrote *Katherine Clausen* and, finally, *Mia Yamaguchi*.

I, for sure, knew who Mia was. Everybody knew Mia. She was easily the most gorgeous girl in school, even as an eighth grader. She wore bangs when nobody else dared wear them, cut straight and low over exotic almond-shaped eyes. Her hair fell like a black velvet cape to her waist and swayed side to side as she walked.

Katherine Clausen was Mia's opposite in nearly every way. Her dishwater blond hair hung in unbrushed clumps around a face so thin and pale I thought she might be sick.

That first day, while we got to know each other and chose Emily Dickinson as our poet, Katherine said only that we should call her Kit. The rest of the time she just chewed on her fingers, her blue eyes watery and unfocused. Ms. Whitcomb said later that we "brought Kit out," and I think we did. At first she just smiled a little more, then laughed. But what really made Kit special was her giggle. A giggle like wind chimes, high and light and contagious. She could make you laugh when things looked their worst. Like we used to say, she was there for us.

But then came boys, and all that changed.

"I wonder if Ms. Whitcomb ever got married." As usual, I'm the first to get to Kit's after school. Elaine's neat little schedule has changed dramatically since she wrote it up. Somehow I ended up with the most shifts. Lunch, after school, *and* dinner. But what can I say? Mia works at Wendy's most nights, and Elaine baby-sits her ninety-year-old grandmother.

Kit and I are on her bed reading *Pride and Prejudice* for English Lit. So far, it's all about getting married, about how to catch the guy with the big bucks, not exactly a book for the nineties as far as I can see.

Kit's stomach doubles as a book rest. "I don't know why I'm reading this," she says. "I'm not going to take the test."

"You're reading it to improve your mind," I say, doing my best Elaine imitation. "Besides, maybe some of it will kind of, like, you know *seep* into him . . . her!"

Kit lays the book facedown on her stomach and frowns. She frowns at her stomach pretty often, like the baby is something that just popped up overnight and surprised her. "Just so it isn't as dumb as me," she says. "Want to feel it kick?" Kit lifts her sweatshirt. Her stretched-out belly gleams. She takes my hand and places it on her right side; then she moves it a little higher. "There," she says. "Feel it?" Nothing. I hold my breath and concentrate. Suddenly I feel something beneath my palm. It's not a kick, at least not like I imagined. It's more of a flutter, like the wings of a butterfly against the walls of a glass jar.

"Oh, wow, yeah," I say, which is about the best I can do. I'm really kind of knocked out. An actual foot, a tiny actual foot.

"Mostly it feels like gas," Kit says, and yawns.

And then I'm kind of embarrassed—I don't know why. It's not about Kit's naked stomach. We've both seen all there is to see of each other, no biggie. And it's not about touching Kit, either. It's just that I suddenly feel like such a kid. I wonder what I'm doing caught up in this thing with Kit, what any of us is doing.

"I'm hungry," Kit says. I'm supposed to jump right up. And I do.

"Yes, Your Royal Highness," I say, but Kit doesn't blink. "PBJs or JPBs?"

"Cut the crusts off, okay?"

"What?"

"I like the crusts cut off—what's wrong with that?"

The kitchen is a mess. Same dishes as three days before, only more of them. I wonder what they do when they run out. Buy more? Somebody's got to do something about it. Three somebodies, the way I figure it. I grab the jars of peanut butter and strawberry jam, the bread, and the last clean knife.

"What does Shirley do around here, anyway? When

she's home, I mean." You have to pass Kit's mother's room on your way to Kit's. The shades are always down, and the bed has never been made as far as I can tell.

Kit's deep into *Pride and Prejudice*, her forehead scrunched up like she just can't figure these crazy women. "Sleeps," she says. "Shirley sleeps. Sleeps and works."

I clear off the dresser and lay out four slices of bread. Kit won't eat anything but the white stuff. They shoot it with vitamins, she says, so it's just as good as the real thing. The peanut butter's my brand, which I won fair and square doing Rock-Paper-Scissors. We both love strawberry jam. Kit will eat it straight out of the jar with her fingers.

The doorbell rings. No matter how many times we tell Elaine not to bother ringing, she does it just the same. "It's just not polite to walk in," she says, miffed, so I've got to run down every time and let her in.

Elaine's waiting patiently, hugging a huge lidded pot. "Spaghetti," she says. "I promised Ma that Kit would eat the whole thing herself." She hands me the pot and drops her backpack on a chair.

"Did you *have* to tell your mother?" I head for the kitchen and stuff the spaghetti in the refrigerator between a month-old carton of milk and an open can of beans growing tiny fur coats.

"Ma? Of course. Did you think I wouldn't?" She sees that I'm frowning. "Oh, don't worry—she won't tell the General. I made her promise on Granddad's grave. How's Kit?"

"Pregnant," I say with a straight face. Elaine rolls her eyes.

"Maybe we should play games or something," she

says, clumping up the stairs behind me. "Get Kit's mind off things. Remember how we used to play Monopoly? For days?"

At the top of the stairs, I turn to face Elaine. She stops on the next step, her round face rosy from carrying the heavy pot all the way from home.

"What?" I don't say anything. "*What?*" Elaine's mom talked her into a perm. Now she looks surprised all the time, like she's been told a shocking story, over and over again.

"Games, Elaine? What about—about *diapers*? What about child support? What about names for the kid? Kit doesn't need Monopoly. She needs a *life!*" Elaine's face crumples. "Well, damn it," I whisper, "I'm the one who's here the most. You guys just don't know. She won't talk about it, about what happens after the baby comes." Only then do I realize how upset I am now that I know who the father is. Why should he get off scot-free? *He* should be baby-sitting Kit. *He* should be making the PBJs.

I turn at the door to Kit's room and give Elaine a quick squeeze. It's not her fault—not a bit of this is her fault.

"Did I hear the word *Monopoly?*" Kit says innocently, but I guess she's heard everything. Elaine and Kit straighten Kit's bed while I run back down the stairs in search of the Clausens' ancient Monopoly game.

Kit's the race car; Elaine's the hat; I'm the shoe. I roll, land on Chance, and Go Directly to Jail. "My turn!" says Kit, full of energy for the first time in weeks. She gets double threes, buys Oriental right off the bat, and rolls again. She's laughing like the old Kit, full of herself in this fantasy world where a roll of the dice can fix you up for life. Maybe Elaine was right. Maybe what Kit needs most is escape.

"I hear you're working on a hot story," Elaine says after a while, skittering the dice across the board. "Top secret stuff." She gets a three and picks up Indiana. She already has Illinois and Kentucky.

"It can't be too secret if you already know about it. What did you hear?" I roll a six, land on St. James, where Kit's stuck three of her little green houses. About the only thing I keep to myself is what I'm working on for the *Taylor Tribune*. It's a matter of professional responsibility, I explain, but Elaine gets put out and I usually end up telling her.

"Yessss!" cries Kit, her blue eyes dancing. "That'll be, let's see, five hundred and fifty dollars!"

"Well, what I heard is that it's about"—Elaine hesitates, glances at Kit, and almost doesn't continue—"abortion."

Kit flips out a flat palm and waits smugly for my rent money.

"Dream on," I tell Elaine, who's always after me to write what I think, do features and not just news. "Would I tackle an issue like that at a school like Taylor? In a town like this?"

Kit looks up. I can tell she's been somewhere else. Like *really* on Park Place. "Whose turn is it?" I pass her the dice.

"So what is it, then? C'mon, tell us. We won't tell. Will we, Kit?"

But Kit's too busy sorting her cash, sticking it in neat piles under the edge of the board. "Huh?"

"It's—" I almost give it away, then change my mind.

Why take the chance of upsetting Kit? Not that I'd use her name. I wouldn't even use her story, though I have to admit it's tempting. I cross my fingers. "It's about . . . about cheating."

"BO-ring," says Elaine.

"Says you." I check my watch. "Where's Mia?"

Kit shrugs. She buys a hotel and plops it on Pennsylvania. "She probably got hung up."

Elaine and I exchange *Yeah, right!* looks. If she's hung up anywhere, it's in a hammock with Mando.

I pay to get out of jail for the sixth time, a real repeat offender. "She could call!"

"Well, you know Mia," Elaine says with an indulgent smile.

I'm getting a little tired of letting Mia off the hook. "Come on, you guys. Stop cutting her slack. It's not fair. Mia thinks about Mia—face it."

"She only missed Monday," Kit says. "And she *did* call."

"Not to mention Wednesday," I add.

Elaine looks up from the board. "What's eating you, Megan? She doesn't do it on purpose. What happened on Wednesday?"

"*She* gets cramps; *I* cut history. It's always something."

"You're so critical, Megan," Kit says. "Nobody's perfect!"

"You *cut?*" Elaine says, like I said I'd murdered someone at lunch. If Elaine cut class, they'd put the flag at half-mast. "We don't cut."

"Yeah, well, we don't do lots of things," I say pointedly.

The doorbell rings. "Well, that's not her." I roll off the bed and head for the stairs. "Mia doesn't ring."

But it is Mia. Mia with a VCR. "Here take this, will you? The TV's still in the car."

I watch her traipse down the walk and open the trunk of her old Barracuda, the hem of her tiny blue sundress swinging side to side. She smiles her Miss America smile coming back up the walk, long brown arm swinging a portable TV.

"Where did you get this?" I was all prepared to give Mia a piece of my mind. Now I don't know what to do with it.

"It's mine," she says. "Don't you recognize it? Mando gave it to me for our anniversary. I thought Kit could use it, you know, at least till the baby comes."

"But what will you do for a TV?" I try to imagine Mia's room without a television. *Any* bedroom without a television. It's unthinkable.

Mia shrugs. "I dunno. What's the difference? Kit needs it more than I do."

I decide to shut my mouth for the rest of the day. That way I can't stuff my foot into it again.

At first I think, *Earthquake!* but it's only Spoofus dreaming. He's chasing cars again, or whatever he does when his back legs get going and the whole bed shakes. I poke him with my foot, and he settles down.

Spoof's been sleeping at the end of my bed since he was a puppy. But now that he's fat and old, he takes up a whole lot more room. It's occurred to me that I might be taller if it weren't for Spoof, but it's his bed as much as it's mine after all these years. Sleeping with bent knees is the least I can do for such an old friend.

The General has had lots to say about all this lying down with dogs of course, but Spoof and I wore her out finally, one of Worfley's "wars of attrition," you might say.

Spoofus wasn't the only one dreaming. I had one going, too. Probably because of cutting Worfley's class. I don't cut as a rule, only in dire emergencies. But these days, considering the state Kit is in, everything seems like an emergency, or at least one in the making. So when Mia begged me to take her shift, I grabbed the cornflakes and the milk and went over to the Clausens' instead of first period. Worfley wouldn't notice, I assured myself with as much confidence as I could gather at a moment's notice. He forgot to take roll all the time and, halfway into the semester, didn't know most of our names.

It's almost morning, and I can't go back to sleep, so I lie there thinking about Joe because thinking about Joe isn't quite as depressing as thinking about Kit. I'm probably not the only girl at Taylor High who wakes up thinking about Joe. He's one of those guys who would have been popular no matter what he looked like because he's got such a great sense of humor. And he *is* cute, even if his nose should have gone to somebody with a bigger face.

I suppose we're broken up, Joe and me, but since I'm not exactly sure we were ever really going together, it's hard to say. The whole thing is one of those "gray areas" my father is always talking about, where nobody can make an "informed" decision because all the facts aren't in. I'm a black-and-white person myself. Either a thing is or it isn't. I suspect Joe's a gray person, though, as is Kit and sometimes Elaine and probably Danny, too. Mia is pure black-and-white. She makes *me* look gray.

I drop back into sleep for a while and wake to the smell of bacon. I pull on my sweats and head for the kitchen. Spoof sleeps on. He can't be bothered, not even for bacon. That's one *old* dog. I wonder sometimes what I'd do without him.

I suppose the General feels the same way about Dad. She's got him pretty freaked out these days about bad cholesterol and the threat of triple bypass surgery, but every now and then he breaks free of her and just goes for it. Eggs are sizzling and popping in the pan. The bacon's ready, a dozen crispy strips side by side on a greasy paper towel. Dad gives me a guilty-as-charged smile and a hug with his free arm. "Over hard?" he asks, though he knows without asking. He flips two eggs, then pokes the yolks, flattening them with his spatula.

We carry our plates to the table. "How are classes going?" he says as always. I watch him go into his routine, tearing off itty-bitty pieces of toast and dropping them onto his sunny-side-up eggs. When he's got the right number of toast pieces, he'll chop the whole thing up and eat it with a dripping spoon. It's so disgusting that I used to set up cereal boxes as a barricade so I couldn't see his plate.

This time when Dad asks his usual, I experience a sudden terrible need to confess. What if Worfley took roll this time? I could write my own excuse—most kids do—but if I get caught at that, I'm doomed. Dad's prosecuting a forger at the moment. He wants to put the poor guy away just for writing a bunch of bad checks. "Don't you see?" he says. "It's not just the money. It's a matter of trust. A man's name has to be worth something. A man's only as good as his word. . . ." And on he goes, winding up like he's in front of a jury. I swallow my confession with my orange juice.

And not a moment too soon. In comes the General. She heads straight for the cupboard, grabs a cup, and pours herself some coffee. She does this mostly by feel since she doesn't have her contacts in yet and refuses to wear glasses, ever. "Up early, aren't you, love?" Dad says.

She gazes across the room in the general direction of his voice. "Mmmm," she says with a nearsighted frown. She brushes my hair back and pecks me on the forehead,

" 'Morning, Megan." Dad makes room for her on his knee, and she settles in with her coffee like a six-year-old sipping hot cocoa. Very un-General-like. At times like this, you think you can get something past her, but you'd be a fool to try.

"There's got to be sixty milligrams of fat just in what you've got left on your plate," the General says. Her hand wanders over to the bacon slices and breaks a tiny bit off a charred end. "I thought you were giving up animal products." She snaps off another piece, a little bigger this time. She puts it in her mouth and licks the tips of her fingers like a cat. She acts like we can't see her doing it, like she's operating in some parallel universe where fat grams don't count.

"When did I say that?" Dad doesn't look as satisfied with his perfect egg concoction as he did before she came in.

"Well, I'm certain you did." I've seen her eat a whole piece of bacon this way, bit by bit. Blatant hypocrisy if you ask me, but if you called her on it, she'd deny it. Right down to the tips of her greasy fingertips. The General would have made a fine politician.

Worfley looks straight at me when I walk into the room. His eyes have a tragic, wounded look to them. My heart does a flip, and the snotty little voice inside that usually keeps me straight says, He knows, he knows. But then his eyes fuzz over, and I realize he's thinking about something else, the Mason-Dixon Line or the '68 Tet Offensive. In Worfley's class you can do your homework for other classes, read a novel, write notes, do a crossword puzzle, just about anything as long as you're quiet. It doesn't seem to matter to him that nobody listens as he goes on and on about his wars. It's as if he has to clarify things for himself, how many boats on the beaches at Normandy, that sort of thing. Once he went on *Jeopardy!* but lost to a housewife from Brooklyn. There wasn't one history question, nothing even close. Worfley gave his home version of *Jeopardy!* to the student center and was kind of a celebrity for about a week.

I settle down in the back of the room with *Pride and Prejudice.* It gets better in the middle. Elizabeth tells Darcy where to get off, which of course hooks him once and for all.

"Megan Lane," Worfley calls, waving a yellow slip. My heart does a back flip. My face is beet red by the time I get to the front of the room, which has gone dead quiet, as if the air's been sucked out. I take the slip with shaking fingers. There's my name all right, but it's not a summons from the office—it's from Mrs. Struthers, the gym teacher. I breathe a sigh of relief and head for the gym. Probably left my lock on a day locker again, no big deal.

My first feature story this year was about girls' sports, which get funded at about a fourth of what goes to the boys. The girls loved it. Harrelson, the head football coach, called my father and, in language he usually reserves for the team, threatened to sue. My father rose to new heights on the telephone that night, pacing back and forth across the kitchen in a passionate defense of my First Amendment rights. That's the night I became a serious features writer. How else can you blab your big mouth like that and get away with it?

I knock on Mrs. Struthers's door. No answer. I knock again. Then, so fast that I can't think, I'm grabbed from behind. There's a hand over my mouth and an arm locked

26

around my waist. I'd scream, if I *could* scream, only the hand tastes like Joe. "You jerk!" I sputter when I've struggled free. "What do you think you're doing?"

"Getting you out of class," he says, palms and eyebrows raised like this is something I forgot we had planned. We're both out of breath from struggling. But Joe's six feet tall. I didn't have a chance.

"Don't ever do that again," I say. "Not to anybody. At least not to a girl." I turn away so he can't see the tears. "You're such a jerk sometimes."

But the more you rag on Joe, the more fun he has. He's grinning, and his molasses brown eyes are so full of life that it's hard not to remember how cute he is, even when he's being a jerk. "Hey, don't go! Come see what I've found," he says. He looks both ways down the hallway and leads me to a room marked EQUIPMENT. He opens the door, and I follow him inside.

There's some light, but not much, coming from a high window at the far end of a room the size of the General's walk-in closet. Stacked on either side are all kinds of balls marked with the name of the school and boxes filled with baseball mitts and jerseys. Someone's hung a gray stretched-out jockstrap from one of the shelves, for decoration I suppose. I stand with my hands on my hips, like the General when she walks into my room. "So?" Joe flips a wrestling mat onto the floor. And then I get it. "You're kidding, Joe. Tell me you're kidding."

"Well, you said not the car," he says. He jumps a couple of times on the mat to check the spring.

This is surreal. What am I doing here? I should be in American History doing my English Lit homework. You can imagine what Elizabeth Bennet would do in a situation like this. Or maybe not. Elizabeth Bennet wouldn't have gotten into this situation in the first place. "And so you searched all over, smart fellow that you are, for a more *romantic* place. I get it. You're nothing if not resourceful, Joe West."

"Hey, thanks!" says Joe, dense as a potato. He plunks down on the mat. "Come here," he says. He pats the mat. "Come on, I won't do anything."

"I can't believe you'd want to," I say, dropping to my knees. "It stinks in here, Joe. It smells like sweaty bodies."

"Let's make sweaty bodies," Joe says, reaching up to meet me, nose to nose. It's amazing how fast your mind can forget everything it ever knew about what your body shouldn't do: the General picking at the bacon, me kissing Joe. Kissing Joe is a whole-body thing, at least it is for me. But the straight little voice in my mind never quite shuts up: if he's this good, it says, he's had some experience. If he's had some experience, who has he had it with? And who did who he had it with, have it with? And so on. It's like looking into one of those mirror things that go on and on and on. It's time for talking, not making out. I pull away from Joe and stumble to my feet. "What are you doing?" says Joe.

"What do you think?" I push my T-shirt back into my jeans, amazed at how fast it got out.

"What did you say the last time?" he says, standing up, still pouting. "After the game?"

"I dunno, what?"

"You said you'd do it but not in the car. So"—his eyes run over the shelves, the light with the burned-out bulb hanging from the ceiling, the wrestling mat bed— "this isn't a car!"

"You've got a memory like Swiss cheese, Joe. What I

said was *Not in the car.* I didn't say I'd do it. I didn't say I'd do it anywhere. That's just the way your mind works."

I grab the doorknob.

"Wait!" Joe says, catching my arm. "Where are you going?"

"History," I say. "Where I should have been all along."

He drops his hand from my arm. "I guess *we're* history, huh?"

Even though I know what I'm doing is right, my heart still sinks. Joe could have just about anybody. Except of course Mia, who's been going with Mando half her life. "I guess we are," I say in my best Elizabeth Bennet, and open the door to the six-foot-three Mrs. Struthers.

"Sorting the equipment?" she says with a cat-and-mouse grin. "Come out here, young man."

We stand before Mrs. Struthers like Adam and Eve. Luckily we've got all our clothes on. "I can explain," Joe says.

"Go ahead," Mrs. Struthers says. She's enjoying this—you can tell. But I know that her philosophy is basically, Kids will be kids. Joe flaps his mouth a little; nothing comes out but wind. "Aw, get out of here, the two of you," she grumbles. "By the way, these walls are made of paper. I could hear you plain as day."

I hurry back to History, wondering how long Mrs. Struthers would have stood outside the door if I hadn't opened it. Makes you think.

I take the long way back to History and end up crossing the lawn in front of the Admin building. I stop and watch the strangest thing. Five women are walking in a circle on the lawn, holding up signs and chanting. Stranger still is that they all look like the General on her way to a board meeting: flower print dresses with lace collars, skirt and sweater sets, matching pumps. "NO CONDOMS ON CAMPUS!" they chant. "NO CONDOMS ON CAMPUS!" Two of the women's faces are bright pink. I glance toward the principal's office and see the Wart peering out through the slats of his miniblinds.

I try to get the attention of a short, squarish woman in lime green polyester. She smiles but won't stop. I try another woman, a serious-looking redhead. She scowls straight ahead without breaking her stride.

"Ladies! Ladies!" cries the Wart, coming across the lawn, suit jacket buttoned, power tie straight. Two of his aides, Mrs. Beamis and Mrs. True, are a good twenty paces behind him and in no hurry to catch up. The Wart waves his arms like he's walking through a bee swarm. His bald head gleams with perspiration. "Ladies! Please, what's going on here?"

The women break their circle. They exchange glances, and the redhead steps forward. "We're CRS," she announces. Even in low-heeled pumps, she towers over the Wart. "Citizens for Responsible Schools. We're putting you on notice."

The Wart looks like he might break a smile. "Notice? You?"

"Yes, us," the redhead says. "And at least a hundred other parents." She looks at her five cohorts for confirmation. "Either you give up your condom distribution program, or we will picket your school until you do."

The women behind her break into a hearty little cheer. "That's telling them, Liz," one says.

"But," says the Wart, "but—ladies! We do not have a condom distribution program at Taylor. Are you sure you have the right school?"

"Oh, yes!" the woman insists. "Your school nurse gave a condom to a young man just last week."

The Wart tries a little humor. "A single condom hardly a distribution program makes. Does it, ladies?" He looks from one to the next. "And you know how students are! How do we know—"

"Oh, we know all right!" the redhead says in an angry burst. "We know because we sent him in to get it!"

The Wart looks decidedly uncomfortable. Sting operations probably aren't covered in his administrator's manual. "Shall we go inside, ladies? Talk this thing over?"

The redhead hesitates, turns to her fellow protesters. They huddle. "All right, Mr. Wartner. We'll come inside. If you're ready to negotiate seriously about this thing."

"Excuse me!" I try the lime green lady again. "Excuse me, but I write for the *Taylor Tribune*, the school newspaper? Do you think I could get an interview?"

The redhead overhears. She turns and pins me. "Who are you?" she says. Then her eyes clear. She almost smiles. "You look like someone . . . I know, Joanna Lane!"

"I'm her daughter, Megan," I say, and offer my hand.

The redhead smiles, impressed with my manners. "Give me a call," she says. "Liz Grant." She rattles off a phone number, and I write it on my hand. "I serve with your mother on Water."

After school I spend way too much time in Video King. Kit's not in the mood for any more stories about resourceful single mothers or talking babies, and I'm not about to watch some gushy romance and beat my breast about Joe. I almost rent *Halloween Thirteen*, but then I think about

Kit's poor baby, who could either come out completely terrified or turn into an ax murderer. I settle for *Serial Mom*.

Kit's in the tub when I get there. Mia is doing her nails; Elaine is reading something that looks like *Webster's Unabridged*. "Don't stay in there too long," I say to the bathroom door. Kit doesn't answer. "Hey! You in there. How long have you been in the tub?"

Mia looks up, then down again at her crimson nails. "Mother's home," she mutters sarcastically.

"How hot is the water?" I go in, and there's Kit with her ears underwater and her eyes closed, naked belly breaking the surface like a floating pink ball. She opens her eyes and gives me a wan smile. "Time to get out," I say, picking a towel up off the floor. She rises from the water like Venus on the half shell, all pink and steamy. Radiant. Just like pregnant women are supposed to be. For a minute I forget the way things are. I forget she's just a kid, that we're just kids. That there's an actual baby inside Kit that flutters its feet like a butterfly. I wrap her in the towel and leave her to dry herself off.

"How do you know all this stuff?" Mia says, blowing on her newly painted nails.

"What stuff?"

"You know, about being pregnant and hot baths and all that."

I shrug. "I don't know. The General, I guess. Must have picked it up."

Mia lays one long, perfect, honey-colored leg on the bed and starts sticking bits of cotton between her toes. "You know, we don't all have to hang around here every day." She says this casually, but I can tell she's been thinking. Time spent with us is time away from Mando.

"So, go." I smooth the sheet on Kit's bed, plump the pillows. A bed always feels better when somebody's plumped the pillows.

Elaine's antenna registers friction. She looks up from her book. "I've got an idea," she says in her peacemaker voice.

"Uh-oh," says Mia.

"Why don't we clean house?" Elaine is just great at looking sweetly innocent. "It won't take the three of us any time at all."

Mia looks at Elaine as if Elaine just announced the ceiling's about to fall. "But I've just done my nails," she says.

"Ta-da!" Elaine pulls three brand-new pairs of yellow Playtex gloves from her backpack and dangles them in the air. "Rubbers!"

I'd never admit it to a soul, but I actually like doing dishes. I like the suds; I like the feel of hot water through the rubber gloves; I like rinsing plates and watching the water glide off in sheets. I think only good thoughts when I'm doing dishes. It goes without saying that the dishes have to be at somebody else's house.

Elaine is tackling the stove with Mr. Clean and a scrub brush. Mia is kind of moving things around, trying not to chip her nails. "Can you imagine this house with a makeover?" She opens one of the cupboard doors and closes it again. The cupboards all have glass windows and glass knobs like tiny prisms. "Maybe we'll buy an older house and fix it up. . . ."

Elaine's already worked up a sweat. "Who, you and Mando?"

"Who else?" Mia has an old-fashioned hope chest in her room. It's from Hawaii, made from the finest koa wood, she says, and stacked with monogrammed white sheets and towels. I didn't know what a hope chest was until she told me, and then I began to wonder: hope for what? For a man? Which gets us back to Elizabeth Bennet. Sometimes I think things haven't changed all that much.

Elaine's been scrubbing nonstop, but the baked-on stuff just won't give up. "Isn't Mando going to med school?"

"Sure," Mia agrees. "What's that got to do with it?"

Elaine's mind and mine are connecting across the room. We know there's trouble in Mia's paradise. Armando Castillo's family has lots to say about what their youngest son, great-grandson of a judge, nephew of a congressman, will do with his life. Mia has been invited to their palatial Spanish adobe only once. Mando's mother asked her a lot of questions about her parents, who were killed in a plane crash when Mia was just a baby. Mia's father was Japanese, her mother Hawaiian. Her ancestors were queens, she says, but Mrs. Castillo wasn't impressed. I guess when your own ancestors go back to the Spanish Inquisition, the Hawaiians seem like new kids on the block.

I work up a sweat scraping out a baking pan. "You guys know if Ms. Adams gives out condoms?"

"I doubt it," Mia says. "She's old."

Elaine strips off her gloves. "What's that got to do with anything?" She wipes her sweaty forehead with the back of her arm. "I'll bet she does. Why? Oh! I know. It's about the protest, right?"

Elaine looks like she's hot on the trail of a story herself. "What are you doing your feature on, Meg? Tell us! It *is* abortion, right?"

"No, it isn't," Mia says smugly. "It's about birth control. Right, Megan? They won't let you print it, you know."

"Well, she shouldn't let that stop her!" Elaine says. "Besides, times change. We didn't have a parenting class before, either."

"Not to mention YMAS." I take three Diet Cokes out of the fridge.

"What's Why-Mass?" Elaine takes a long swallow and chokes.

Mia thumps Elaine's back. "Where have you been? YMAS. Young Mothers at School. The Incubating Center."

"Mia!" The General's on the school board, of course. They approved YMAS by a narrow margin, 4–3. All we heard at home for about three months was YMAS. Was it encouraging young mothers to finish their education, or was it just making it easier for children to have children?

"Well, it *is* an incubating center! It's like this club or something. I've heard that girls get pregnant on purpose, just so they can be with their friends."

Elaine can't believe her ears. "You're making that up!"

My mind is incubating. The story is coming together faster than I can write it.

"How about a cup of herb tea?"

"Uh-uh," says Kit—not even a thanks. She's in a rotten mood. She's tired of staying in bed all day, she says. It's only been two weeks, she says. How is she going to stand it for two whole *months*? Her back hurts; her head aches; her feet are swollen up like melons. She goes on and on. It's awful, but all I can think of is *The Exorcist*. In her rumpled flannel nightgown, with her stringy hair hanging in her face, Kit could be Linda Blair's understudy.

I stoop to pick Kit's robe off the floor. Her rug is full of cat hair. Cat hair and dust float slowly through the lazy morning sunlight. "Mind if I run the vacuum?"

Kit frowns. "Whatever turns you on."

I bite my tongue. Lately I've been biting my tongue a lot. I have to remind myself constantly how I would feel if I were in Kit's place. But I'm not exactly Mother Teresa. One of these days Kit will go too far, and I'll pop off. Then of course I'll feel terrible.

I locate the Clausens' ancient Hoover in a downstairs closet and haul it up the stairs. The General wouldn't believe this, her daughter actually vacuuming without being asked. At home, nothing really needs doing. The General has it all under control. We don't use the living room except for guests, but it gets vacuumed every week anyway. It looks like one of those rooms in a museum that have been moved piece by piece from some famous place and perfectly preserved for posterity. It's no coincidence, given the General's profession, that the whole house is 100 percent germfree. Once I caught her doing bathroom corners with Q-Tips.

Here at the Clausens', it's another story. You could pick a room and spend a week just restoring it to normal. I run the vacuum over Kit's rug and consider doing Shirley's rug a similar favor. But Shirley's stuff's all over the floor.

The Hoover has a bad case of asthma. It wheezes but hangs on till I'm finished. I thump it down the stairs and stow it in the closet. Back in Kit's room, I gather up the remains of last night's pizza, and that's when I notice the cigarette butt. I pick it up between fingernail tips. "Mia isn't smoking around you, is she?"

Kit looks up from the latest *Glamour* (I bought her a copy of *Parents*, but she has yet to open it). "That's not Mia's."

"Oh? Then whose?"

Kit flips a page and is suddenly terribly interested in "Toning and Trimming for Summer Fashions." Kathy Ireland struts across the page in a pair of skimpy cutoffs. *If a new mom can do it,* the caption says, *so can you! Ten Tips To Get You There in Style.*

"It's yours? You smoked this?"

Kit tosses *Glamour* aside. There are dark circles under her eyes, and I wonder if she's been sleeping. "Meg, can I tell you something?"

"Yeah."

"Promise you won't feel bad."

"How can I promise when I don't know what you're going to say? Be real."

"Then I can't say it."

I roll my eyes. "Give me a break, Kit." She's biting skin off her bottom lip. "Okay, I promise."

"It's just that . . . well, you're always on my case lately." She looks at the neutral gray eye of Mia's television instead of at me. "You're in a bad mood all the time—"

"Me? *I'm* in a bad mood?"

"It's like you want to be my mother or something. You just, like, *take over.*" She risks a peek at me, and I can see how hard this has been for her to say. Still, I feel like I've been kicked in the stomach. I kneel to pick up a caved-in Coke can. The white letters wave like they're underwater. I blink back tears, pretending to gather more junk. By the time I stand up, I've got myself under control.

"I'm sorry, Meg," Kit says, biting on her thumb. "It's not *you.* Really. You do so much for me—I don't know why I said that. I'm sorry." She holds out her hand. I ignore it.

"Hey!" I say, upbeat as anything, but I can feel my neck heating up. "You're right. I mean, it's not as if you *need* help. You're just flat on your back pregnant, with no money, no food, no *future!*" Inside, the voice of my better self says, Slow down, Megan Lane, slow down. But it's too late. I'm on a roll. "And a useless mother besides!

Hell, no, you don't need help. Pardon me for thinking you ever did!" I grab my backpack and sling it over my shoulder. "*If* you need anything, call Mia. See how fast *she* gets here!"

Kit struggles to sit up. She looks just like I've slugged her. I leave her looking like that, like the devil's just whipped through her room.

I stop at the oak tree, halfway between Kit's house and mine. In the "old days," Kit and I used to walk each other halfway, exactly to this tree. We were in our ugly phase then. I grew four inches overnight and towered over everybody like a redheaded giraffe. Kit said I was just growing into a model, and for a while I believed her. She told me I was the smartest person she ever knew and the best friend a girl could have. She said if nobody else wanted us (meaning boys), at least we'd have each other. Kit was petite and I envied that, but her normally colorless face began to erupt in bright red zits. "Pizza face," some jerk said at school, and Kit ran home crying. We'd talk on the phone for hours, telling each other great things neither of us really believed but needed desperately to hear. Bad as they seemed then, I'd bring those days back if I could. I'd make Kit think about the choices she was going to make. I'd be sure she didn't make stupid ones. Somehow.

I lean my forehead against the rough bark of our tree. One part of me knows that Kit is right: I've been taking over just like the General would. But I'm hurt and angry, too. Haven't I always been there for Kit? Isn't that what it means to be Friends Till the End? And what if somebody changes? What if they stop being who you thought they were? Friends till the end is a long, long time.

Dad and I flip a coin for where we'll go to dinner. He likes All-You-Can-Eat, I like Pasquali's, where Joe works as a busboy. Dad wins. We both eat too much and go home groaning. I go up to bed, set the clock for midnight. By then the General will be home and asleep. I put the clock under my pillow, but I can't sleep. I'm too full of food and guilt. A little before twelve, I sneak down the hall and head for Kit's.

Elaine's VW is parked in front of Kit's house when I get there, and I almost turn back. I don't exactly feel like apologizing to Kit in front of anybody, even though I know Elaine would understand. Everybody in her family blows up. Everybody but Elaine. It's normal for Italian families, she says, even healthy.

Kit's room is dark. Kit and Elaine are eating popcorn in the gloomy gray light of *Casablanca*. It's nearly over, and Rick is saying all the noble things to Ilsa about going on without him. "We'll always have Paris," he says. Tears are running down Ilsa's face, down Elaine's and Kit's faces, too. They weep silently, stuffing the popcorn in, all at the same time. There's a roll of toilet paper between them on the bed. I have to laugh—it's just too much.

"Shhh!" They don't even glance my way. The plane chuffs down the runway. Rick turns away. He saunters off into the darkness with Captain Renault.

"Oh, God," says Elaine, and blows her nose into a wad of toilet paper. "That's the most beautiful ending!" She turns on the light and gets up to rewind the tape.

"We thought you were Mia," Kit says as if nothing's happened. Kit doesn't hold a grudge. It's one of her best traits. I could throw my arms around her right now, but we'd both be embarrassed.

"It's just Mother Lane," I say. "Is there butter on that popcorn? I hope you didn't oversalt it! Salt's bad for babies, you know."

"Give it up, Megan," Kit says, and things are back to normal.

"You're just in time," Elaine says, plopping back onto the bed with her purse. "I brought this little book." She fishes through her purse and pulls out *Alexandra to Zed: Naming Your Baby.* "You don't want to wait until the last minute. Some relative always steps in with something awful, something dreadful, like Mildred."

"That's my grandmother's name!" I say, poker-faced.

Elaine sucks her breath in. Her big brown eyes are wide and tragic. "Oh, it isn't, Megan. Is it? Oh, God, I'm sorry."

"Mildred Gertrude Frieda Dagmar Lane." Kit's got her hand over her mouth to keep from busting up.

"Wow, that's some name," Elaine says reverently.

"Oh, *Elaine!*" Kit and I say together.

"You *guys!*"

Elaine reads some of the better names in the book aloud. "Alanna, Alessandra, Alicia . . ."

"Nothing old-fashioned," I say. "Right, Kit? Nothing biblical." But Kit's not into it. She's into *Glamour.* Into picturing herself strolling on the beach with Kathy Ireland. After a while Elaine and I run out of steam.

"Well, I'll just leave this for you to look at," Elaine says lamely. She places the little book on Kit's bedside table.

The door slams downstairs. "Mia?" says Elaine.

"Shirley," Kit says grimly.

"It's not closing time, is it?" Then I hear another voice, a man's voice.

"There probably wasn't any business," Kit says. I can tell by the look in her eyes that she's listening to the other voice, too. "Don't go yet, you guys. Okay?"

Shirley and whoever it is are laughing downstairs, the loose laughter of too many drinks. Then footsteps, one pair by the sound of it.

"Why, it's the whole troop!" Shirley says, bursting into the room. Her breath is a knockout combination of Jack Daniel's and Camel Lights. Kit and I know all about it. We used to sneak cigarettes from her pack, and once we drank enough of her whiskey to see what it felt like to be Shirley. Not good, not good at all. "Woops, no," hiccups Shirley. "Not the whole troop, after all. Where's Miss Hawaii?" She doesn't wait for an answer, not that she was going to get one. "How are you, my love?" she says, hovering over Kit, who's got her frozen face on. She pulls the blankets up and tucks them in around Kit, just like a real mother would. "Poor baby, staying in bed all day long without her mama to take care of her!" She leans down to kiss Kit, wobbling on her platforms. Kit turns her head, catching the kiss on her ear. "Well!" says Shirley brightly, hands on her hips, surveying the room with glazed-over eyes and smeared mascara. Her lipstick's smeared, too. I try to picture the guy downstairs, then change my mind.

"You girls have been just super," Shirley says with all the drunken sincerity she can muster. "Keeping my Kit company like you do." She weaves a little left and right. "Well . . . ," she says.

"Good-night, Ma," Kit says to the wall.

Shirley looks confused for a minute. "Oh, well, yeah," she says. "I'll leave you girls alone. I know about girl talk—don't think I don't!" She gives us a little wave with the curled tips of her fingers like she's about thirteen years old and wobbles out of the room. Sometimes I almost feel sorry for Shirley—I don't know why. It's a look she gets in her eyes, like she really wants to make things work better than they do but doesn't know where to start.

"Want us to stay?" Elaine looks like she can't wait to get out of the house.

"No, it's okay," Kit says. "Just sneak out, okay? That way she'll think you're still here."

Elaine and I lean against her VW, looking up at the Clausens' house. It doesn't look like a place where anybody could ever be happy.

"Kit used to sing," Elaine says quietly. "Remember that?"

I smile. "She was going to be the next Patsy Cline."

"But first she was going to save all the stray cats in the world and put them on her own private island."

"Was that before or after acting school?"

"Before acting school, after the Peace Corps."

"What happened, Elaine?"

"To Kit? I don't know. Something. She's different, isn't she? Like she's not connected anymore. To us, or to anything."

I'm making out with Joe, and the phone is ringing off the hook. Joe says it can't be ringing, that we're on a sailboat in the middle of the Pacific. I wake up, sad to let Joe drift away. He's even better in dreams than in real life. "Hello?" My sleepy voice cracks, so I try again. "Hello?"

"Meg? Mia." I can hardly hear her. I transfer the phone to my left ear, hoping it's more awake. "Listen, I can't get to Kit's this morning. Meg? Are you there?"

"I'm here. Where are *you*?" I hear what sounds like a semi whiz by. Mia doesn't answer for a minute. I listen to the traffic. It doesn't sound like the local kind. "Mia, where are you? Bakersfield?"

I expect her to laugh, but she doesn't. Our standard joke for years is that we'll end up housewives in Bakersfield. "I dunno," she says. "Somewhere north. Look, I'm sorry, but you've got to take the breakfast shift at Kit's. I took a drive to think, and, well, I went too far—that's all."

"But I can't cut History again." Another truck rumbles by. "Mia, what's wrong?"

"I can't talk about it on the phone. Don't worry, okay? I'm all right. Really. It's just—it's just something with Mando. Will you do it? Will you go to Kit's? We can't ask Elaine to cut—you know that." For once I think, Kit can get her own damned cereal. What's so bad about that? What's so bad is that we said we'd be there, one of us. We're only as good as our word, etc., etc.

"Okay," I grumble into the phone. "Call me, will you? Call me as soon as you get back. Even if I'm not home yet. Leave a message." The phone line hums between us. "Mia?"

"Yeah?"

"Be careful. Like, don't give anybody a ride or anything."

"As if I would." For a minute she sounds like the regular Mia. The phone goes dead, and I realize she's hung up without saying good-bye.

There's no point in worrying Kit or the baby. I tell Kit that Mia's car's broken down again. Mia drives an ancient Plymouth Barracuda, one of the last known Barracudas in the modern world. When it breaks down, you have to do cross-species transplants. Highly technical. Only a few mechanics in the country can do them.

Kit and I are careful with our moods this morning. I'm terribly charming, and she's terribly grateful. "Oh, *thank you*, Meg," she says. "This is just the way I like my cornflakes." Which is how? With milk? There aren't many ways to mess up a bowl of cornflakes. "You're welcome, Kit. Is there anything else you need?"

And then we relax into our normal selves. "So what's with Joe these days?" Kit pokes halfheartedly at her corn-flakes and finally chews up half a spoonful.

"Who knows? One minute I think he's really into me; the next . . . who knows?" I stretch out next to Kit, thinking how easy it would be to drift back out into the Pacific.

Kit sets her cereal, half-finished, on the nightstand. "You know how we used to say the guys just want one thing?" Kit says. "Remember? We thought we were so cool, that we had that all figured out."

"And?"

"Well, it's just not that simple, is it? I mean, that's what Monk wanted. That's fairly obvious." She grimaces at her midsection. "But some guys have got to be, I don't know, more . . . well-rounded than that. Sex isn't all *we* talk about."

"No? Like what are we talking about at the moment? Shakespeare? Nuclear physics? Let's face it, Kit. We think about sex just as much as the guys do."

"But it isn't all we want, is what I'm saying. I mean we don't exactly *obsess* on it!"

I think about Joe and the equipment room. And then I wonder about Kit and Monk, where they did it and all that. But it seems—I don't know . . . indelicate to ask, because Kit got pregnant. The giggle's gone out of every-thing. Still, I can ask Kit things I could never ask Mia. And then I'm worrying about Mia, about what's gone wrong. I feel like a mother hen sometimes, but I just can't help it. "Can I ask you something?"

"Sure."

"Did you, I don't know . . . *like* it with Monk? I mean, you did it more than once, right? You didn't get, you didn't—"

"Get knocked up the very first time?" Kit's propped up against her pillows. She looks down at me lying next to her. She knows I'm going to react.

"That's terrible, Kit. I hate that expression. I don't think the baby should hear that kind of language." It's strange, but sometimes I think I worry more about this baby than Kit does.

"Yeah, right," Kit says dryly.

"I'm serious! You yourself said that you remembered your father walking out the door when you were just a baby. How do we know *this* baby doesn't hear everything we say?"

"Then maybe we shouldn't be talking about sex." Kit laughs.

"Get real. If somebody talked to us, maybe this wouldn't have happened."

"To me, you mean. You don't think Shirley told me about sex? She told me about everything. From French kissing to condoms."

"But that's like, I don't know . . . the *mechanics*." I sit up, prop Kit's teddy bear behind my back. She's slept with Mr. Bear so long, it doesn't even seem strange anymore. "That's the way it was in health class, remember? 'Okay, you guys, here's what you do and here's how you do it, but don't you *dare* do it!' "

"Well," Kit says, remembering, "I guess it was better than nothing. Most kids know zip."

"Not to change the subject, but SATs are next Friday. Are you going to take them?"

Kit looks surprised, another reminder that she's a long way from school these days, even though she's doing the work I bring home for her. "Yeah, I mean, I *want* to. But not like *this*." Taking SATs means you're seriously heading for college. Has she thought any of this through? How can she go to college with a baby to take care of? And how will she pay tuition and all the rest of it? Her grades are good, but not good enough for scholarships.

I jog the whole way back to school, but I'm five minutes tardy just the same. Ms. Sato gives me a sour look but doesn't send me back to the office for a pass. I'm itching to get through class and back to the article. Ms. Adams has promised me an interview. I figure if anybody knows anything about what kids are up to, it's her.

I explain to Ms. Adams that I'm doing a story for the *Trib* on birth control. She is the last of her kind, a school nurse on duty in a high school. But she volunteers her time, and nobody has the heart to let her go. She's ancient, but her tongue's as sharp as ever. She sits down and curls her hands in her lap. She sighs. I think for a minute that she isn't going to be an easy interview. "Well, it's a terrible thing, isn't it?" she says. "What young people are doing to themselves these days. Gambling with their future. Having babies when they're just babies themselves. . . ."

"Terrible," I agree. "Mind if I tape?"

"Oh," she says, and looks at my tape recorder as if something so tiny couldn't be real. "I suppose you want to know if it's true," she says.

I feign ignorance. "If what's true?"

"Well, if I'm the one who's handing out the condoms." Her face is old, but her eyes are clear and blue as a child's.

"Are you?"

"Well, of course I am. Who do you think would do it if I didn't?"

I'm so surprised at her admission that I can't think of what to say next.

"And that's not all I dispense," she says. "No condom goes out of here without a good piece of my mind."

"Oh?"

"All they've got on their minds is sex!" she says vehemently. "Why, there's a whole world out there! Opportunities I never had. Education! Travel! Just how far do they think they can get with a baby on their back? About as far as the grocery store—that's what. For disposable diapers. Which they can't afford! I tell them, 'Here, take this.' " She reaches into a drawer and takes out a foil-wrapped condom. "I say, 'Keep it in your pocket or your purse. Just in case.' "

"You mean they don't come in asking for them?"

"Some of them do, yes. And some come in when it's too late. They come in crying that they've missed a period, two periods." She shakes her head. "What do they think? Does anybody talk to them about planning their lives? Algebra isn't going to help—let me tell you!"

I head on over to the *Trib* room and jump on the computer.

Teen Sex (DRAFT)

"Nothing in the forty-six years that I've been a nurse has prepared me for what's going on in high schools today," says Ms. Harriet Adams, Taylor's school nurse. "It's as if the kids are wearing blindfolds and earplugs. Don't they know how they're risking their futures and, worse, their lives?"

Here are just a few of the reasons Ms. Adams is concerned: 54% of high school students in the U.S. (61% of boys and 48% of girls) say that they have had sexual intercourse, according to a 1992 Centers for Disease Control study. Each year, 1 of every 10 teenage girls becomes pregnant, and more than 400,000 teenagers have abortions. Approximately 65% of sexually transmitted diseases (STDs) are found among teenagers, some of them resulting in sterility or even in death. In the past two years, AIDS among 14- to 23-year-olds has gone up 72%.

At home I expect to hear Mia on the answering machine, but no luck. I find the General in her bathroom, putting on her makeup. It's fascinating to watch her—she's so precise. Probably should have been a surgeon instead of just a nurse. *Just* a nurse. She'd have my head for that.

I look at both of us in her vanity mirror. We look alike. Too much alike. Her curly hair is short and more blond than red (with help) but we're built pretty much the same way: no boobs to speak of, long skinny legs and arms, broad shoulders, no earlobes. I guess you could say our looks are about average, though Dad says we are both exceptionally beautiful women. Cracks me up every time.

"What are you thinking about?" In four deft, perfect strokes, the General's got her lip liner in place.

"Nothing much." Not true. I can't look at her and not think about IT.

"Dad says you're spending a lot of time at Elaine's these days."

"He does?"

"Well, every time I call, you're out." Her eyes shift to mine. Her lashes are double-coated and spiky. "Or is it Joe you've been spending so much time with? You know our rule about dates on school nights." She fills in the lines of her lips with coral lipstick.

"Nope. No Joe." It feels good to be telling something close to the truth for a change.

The General pokes and pushes at her curls. She grabs the can of hair spray. I back out of range. "You're frowning again," she says.

"No, I'm not." I frown at my reflection. She blasts her hair with a cloud of chemicals.

"You worry too much, Megan. You're going to give yourself an ulcer."

"I know. I just can't help it."

"Worrying doesn't change things."

My eyes and nose fill up. The General frowns. "There's something bothering you, isn't there? Something you're not telling me."

What would she say if I told her about Kit? That Mia's disappeared? That I've cut History twice so far?

Instead, I shake my head. "PMS," I say, and grab a wad of tissue to blow my nose.

*　*　*

The General leaves for work, and Mia calls. "Sorry, kiddo," she says. "I've been sleeping all day. I drove to San Francisco. Well, almost. Then I turned around and drove all the way back."

"In the 'Cuda? You're lucky you didn't break down somewhere."

"Mando called it quits, Meg," she says, her voice flat as roadkill.

I can't believe what I'm hearing. Mia and Mando are like the moon and stars, fixed in space, eternal. I say the predictable stupid things, one after another. "You're kidding. I can't believe it. No way!" Babbling. But I really can't absorb this.

"Look." Mia sighs. "I'm exhausted. I'll see you tomorrow, okay? I'll tell you all about it."

"We'll go to the mall," I say, and I know that Mia understands. It's all I can think of to offer. Shopping can't cure a broken heart, but it can make you forget you have one for at least a little while.

6

"I can't eat this stuff," Mia says.

The South Plaza Mall's gone international. Italian, Chinese, Vietnamese, Indian—you name it, they cook it. Mia's got a paper plate full of some lumpy yellowish concoction, poured over an ice-cream-scoopful of gluey rice. We both know that the reason she can't eat is Mando.

"Maybe this wasn't such a good idea after all," she says. Crowds of happy campers cruise the mall, moms pushing strollers, dads packing newborns in kangaroo-like pouches. It's Saturday, and everybody's out. A tiny girl with golden ringlets toddles past our table. She waves shyly, and my heart melts. Mia's already named the kids she would one day have with Mando—that's how sure she was.

"I guess you're right." I stand and gather up our paper plates and cups to toss them in the trash. "Where to? We could take a run. Do something active." I haven't jogged in over two weeks, not since Kit's latest development, which changed the way we've been living our lives. My thighs are jellying out.

"Nope," Mia says, tossing her hair decisively over her shoulder. "We came to get shower stuff. Let's do it."

"You really want to look at baby clothes?"

"Sure, why not?"

"That tells me something, Mia," I say as we head out of the food court toward Penny's Hallmark and Chicken Little, "where only the prices are falling."

"What, O wise one?"

"That you haven't really given up. On Mando, I mean."

Mia doesn't answer right away. She's watching the tips of her flip-flops, as if she has to keep them both in a straight line. Then she sighs and looks over at me. "How can I, Meg? He promised." Her eyes sparkle with tears. "He said it was forever. I know he meant it. I *know* he did."

If I were Elaine, I'd put an arm around Mia right now. Elaine doesn't care who wonders about her sexual preferences. She's above all that. My hands won't come out of my pockets. "What changed his mind? His parents? Did his mother finally get to him?"

We pause to finger the merchandise on the sale table in The Limited. Same old stuff. "He says not, but they never stopped putting the pressure on him, you know? What he *says* is that he doesn't want to tie me down for my senior year. Can you believe that? How unselfish!" She laughs shortly. "Yeah, right. It's all for me." Anger keeps her tears in check, and for a few minutes she's almost her take-no-prisoners self again.

In Penny's Hallmark, Mia and I buy napkins and paper plates, balloons and crepe paper for the shower. We stick pretty much to green and yellow, though secretly we're all hoping for a girl. *All* meaning Mia, Elaine, and me. Kit hasn't said one way or the other.

"Mia, do you think Kit's going to be a good mother?"

Mia glances at me out of the corner of her eye. "Are you serious?"

"Well, kind of, yeah. I mean, can you see a baby in that house? Kit forgets to feed the cats about half the time, and the place is—well, you know how it is. Not to mention Shirley. How would you like to have her for a grandma?"

"I try not to think about it," Mia says, but I know she does. She has dozens of nieces and nephews in Hawaii, where children, she says, are cherished. "What can we do, anyway?"

I sidestep a loose Rottweiler trailing a leash. "I dunno. Something."

"Yeah, well, think about it for a minute, Meg. You know Kit. She counts on us for everything, always has. In some funny way, I think she sees this baby as all of ours."

Mia's put in words what's been creeping around the edges of my mind. I don't want a baby. Not even part-time. I feel a little like a traitor, but my life's been mostly Kit's for weeks now. I'm starting to miss being just me.

And then, sometimes, when I'm really off guard, I can almost feel what it would be like to rock a little pink bundle that looks just like Kit. I wonder, Am I in control of my biology or is biology in charge of me? It's more than a little scary.

"She probably just figures we'll keep coming over, round the clock," Mia says. "Elaine takes the two A.M. feeding; Mia makes the formula at dawn; Meg runs over at the drop of a diaper pin for whatever, whenever!" She pats my shoulder as if to say that I'm a little nutty when it comes to Kit, but that she likes me, anyway.

"We should discuss this." I sound like the General at a school board meeting. "Find out just what's on Kit's mind. She still doesn't talk about it. Doesn't say a word about the baby, even when I bring it up. Don't you think that's—I dunno—a little strange?"

"Kit? Strange?" says Mia with a laugh. "Whatever gave you that idea?"

"After the shower, that would be a good time." We head across the parking lot toward the Barracuda.

"For what?" Mia's got her glazed-over look back, and I know she's thinking about Mando again.

"What do you think? To talk to Kit. To make plans. You just can't have a baby and go on with your life like nothing's happened."

"Oh no? I'll bet Kit can!"

Sunday, ten till four. Kit's house is quiet as an empty box. I figure Shirley's sleeping, so I'm quiet going up the stairs and down the hall to Kit's room. Kit's curled up on her side, asleep, arms around Mr. Bear. Her face is flushed, and her mouth is open. In sleep, Kit always looks like she's fighting something or having terrible dreams. She looks about seven years old and completely defenseless. I touch her shoulder, and her eyes flip open. "The shower starts at four," I remind her. "Don't you want to clean up?"

Kit closes her eyes. I pull the cord on the ancient blinds. They inch up with a lot of rusty complaining. Sunlight floods the room, and I'm amazed at what a mess one bedridden person (and a few friends) can make. "Damn it, Meg," Kit says, throwing an arm over her eyes. "Can't you let me sleep?"

"That's all you do all day, Kit."

"That's what I'm supposed to do," she grumbles. She rolls over on her side and pulls herself slowly into a sitting position. Her belly seems to expand now by the day, and everything she does, every move she makes, seems to cost her air.

"The doctor said to stay off your feet, not zone out. The baby needs stimulation." I flick on the radio. Pearl Jam—not exactly Mozart.

"Says the famous Dr. Lane." Kit leans forward and picks something out from under her big toenail. She's been wearing the same nightgown for weeks.

"Well, we're in a pleasant mood, aren't we? Get up out of there!"

Kit looks up from her toes. "Huh?"

"Get out of there. I'm going to change your sheets."

"Jeez, Megan. It's just us girls."

"Don't give me any lip. Besides, Elaine's mother's coming, and she's almost as picky as the General. Why don't you take a shower? I've brought something for you to wear."

Kit says The Word We Do Not Say under her breath, slides out of bed, and waddles down the hall toward the bathroom. I grab the roll of crepe paper and the Scotch tape out of my backpack. I loop it from one end of the room to the other and back again. I'm blowing the last of the balloons when Kit comes back, her hair hanging in wet strings. "Oh, Meg," she says, "you're too much!" But I can see she's pleased.

I help Kit into one of the General's slinky nighties.

It's pale blue with bands of lace and brings out the color in Kit's eyes. I hold the matching robe for her to slide into. She ties it around her middle. "There," she says, looking pleased with herself for the first time in months. "How do I look?"

"Beautiful, Kit," I say. "Beautiful." And it's true.

"Surprise!" Elaine bursts into the room, for once without knocking at the front door. She's got a bottle of champagne, genuine French stuff. "Oh, well, I guess it isn't really a surprise. Kit! You look so pretty!" She hands me the champagne and throws her arms around Kit, who's blushing. Elaine's mom is carrying a yellow frosted cake on a crystal cake plate, complete with silver pedestal. She looks around for a place to set it down. "Is your mother home?" She glances suspiciously around the room, as if guessing that Shirley might just jump out of the closet straight onto the cake. She doesn't know Shirley all that well, but she knows *about* Shirley.

"*Ma!*" Kit bawls. No answer.

Mia appears with the presents wrapped in their happy baby paper. For some reason, she's wearing black, one of those stretchy little dresses only someone like Mia can get away with. I figure she's in mourning. Why else would she wear black to a baby shower? "Your mother says quit yelling—she's coming," Mia says, setting the presents down at the end of Kit's bed. "How pretty you look, Kit!"

We all stand around Kit's bed in an uncomfortable silence. Then Mia says, "Well, let's have a toast!" She peels the foil from the champagne and untwists the little wire cage that holds the cork. The cork pops, and in comes Shirley, right on cue. "Oh, Kitten," she says, waving an unlit Camel toward the balloons and streamers. "Isn't this the nicest thing! You girls have simply outdone yourselves. Anybody got a match?" Nobody answers. "Oh, well, I guess nobody's smoking, huh? Bad, bad." She tucks the cigarette into her cleavage. "Mom's being a bad girl, isn't she, Kitten?" But Kit's busy pretending her mother's not there.

Mia passes around plastic glasses half-filled with champagne. Kit gets ginger ale and makes a face. "A toast," Mia says. And I realize how proud I am of her for putting her own sadness aside. It's hard not to wonder if Kit would do the same for her. For any one of us. She's never had to. She's always been the baby. And we've let her be one. "Here's to Kit," Mia says. "May all your problems be little ones."

We touch our plastic glasses in a toast. Shirley downs hers in a single swallow. "We haven't even thought of names yet," she says. "Have we, sugar?" Kit doesn't answer. "Well!" she says with a too-bright smile. "Isn't this just the nicest thing?" She pokes at her copper curls, shifts from one platform shoe to the other. You can see how badly she wants that cigarette. "Isn't that the sweetest cake?"

"Speaking of which . . . ," Elaine says, grabbing the cake cutter. She looks relieved to have something to do. "It's carrot cake," she says. "Mom makes the absolute best!"

"Kit should open her gifts first," Elaine's mother says. "Besides, Elaine, you know the cake's from a box." She looks around and shrugs. Her chins wobble as she laughs. "Who has time to make from scratch?"

Shirley chuckles sympathetically, as if she, too, has had to resort to making all her cakes from a mix. Shirley's been known to ruin Jell-O.

"Okay," Mia says to Kit, "open your presents."

For the first time, Kit looks truly uncomfortable. But she reaches for one of the boxes and slowly begins to peel away the paper. She actually looks as if the box might blow up in her hands. Even I don't know what to make of this.

"Do that thing with the string, Ma," Elaine says suddenly.

"What thing with the string?" Elaine's mother rests her big arms on the summit of her huge belly. If she weren't almost fifty, you'd think the shower was for her.

"Oh, you know. Remember? What you did with cousin Lydia's wedding ring when she was carrying Tito."

"Oh. . . ." Elaine's mother looks a little unsure. "Maybe Kit doesn't want to know whether it's a boy or a girl. Do you, Kit?"

Kit folds the baby paper in smaller and smaller squares. I wonder why she's gotten so neat all of a sudden. "Well . . ." She looks around at the three of us girls. "If you all want to know . . . I guess . . ." She shrugs.

"Do it, Ma!" Elaine coaxes. "Here, you can use this ribbon." She passes her mother the yellow ribbon from Kit's gift. "Oh!" she says, suddenly embarrassed. "No ring, huh?" She slips off the silver friendship ring I gave her for her birthday. "Here," she says, "this will work, won't it? I mean, it doesn't *have* to be a wedding ring. . . ."

We all watch as Elaine's mother dangles the ring at the end of the yellow ribbon over Kit's belly. Nothing happens for a minute or two. Then the ring starts to circle. "A girl," she pronounces. "I hope that's what you want."

"Sure," Kit says, but she doesn't sound at all convincing.

"Well, that's a relief!" Mia says. "Who needs a man around here anyway?"

Silence.

"Oh, cute," Kit says when she's finished unwrapping the first box. She holds up a miniature version of Mr. Bear. One by one, she goes through all the gifts. Elaine snaps pictures of everything and everyone, even Shirley, who is sipping the last of the champagne straight from the bottle.

"I thought I'd wait, you know, until I see what she really needs . . . ," Shirley says when it's obvious to all of us that there's nothing for the baby from its grandmother.

"Good idea!" says Elaine's mother generously. "You never know until the baby's born. You always get so much. . . ." We can't help but glance at the meager pile of gifts on Kit's bed. "Cake, everybody?"

After the shower, when it's just the four of us again, Kit seems edgy. One minute she's chattering like some jungle bird; the next she's silent as stone. Mia and Elaine are sitting on the floor. Each has a second piece of cake, a big second piece. I'm on the bed putting the baby stuff back into boxes. Kit's quiet for a long time. Then she says in that tentative way she has, "You guys?"

Mia and Elaine look up from their cake. Something in her voice has caught my attention, too.

"I've got something to tell you. . . ."

"Oh, God, no," Mia says. "It's twins."

"Not funny," says Elaine.

Kit ignores them both. "I hope you won't be too disappointed—"

"What?" The three of us with one voice.

"I've decided, well, I've decided to do something you might not exactly agree with."

Finally Elaine says very carefully and quietly, as if she's talking to a child or a mental patient, "It's too late for an abortion, Kit."

"Of course it's too late," Kit says. "What do you think? I'm stupid?"

"Then, what?" says Mia. I'm not talking—I don't know why. I just don't like the feel of this.

"I'm not going to keep this baby," she says.

Nobody moves. Nobody even blinks.

"I'm giving it up," she says, "for adoption."

Silence. I look at Mia; Mia looks at Elaine. We all look at Kit like she's grown three heads.

"I mean, what would I do with a baby?" Kit starts to cry. She throws out her arms dramatically. "What kind of life is this for a baby?"

Mia clears her throat. Elaine says quietly, "Oh, wow."

"You're giving the baby away?" I say the words, just to have them out there once and for all.

"You don't have to put it that way," Kit says, wiping her nose with the edge of the sheet. "It's not like I'm going to sell it or something. There's this couple," she says. "They've been trying and trying to have a baby for years. . . ."

I get up and walk to the window, look down on the weed-choked front lawn. "How long have you known about this?"

Kit doesn't answer.

Mia gets to her feet, puts her half-eaten piece of cake

on the dresser. "I don't think I can talk about this right now," she says.

"Mia?" Elaine scrambles to her feet and follows Mia out the door. She comes back alone.

"It's the best thing, you guys," Kit says. "Don't you see?" The tears roll down her face, down the front of the General's blue nightie. Both Kit's hands are stretched across her belly as if, without her even knowing it, she's talking to the baby, not to us.

Elaine sits on the edge of the bed and takes Kit in her arms. Kit sobs against Elaine's shoulder.

"What I don't understand," I say quietly, like I'm trying to reason with the faded wallpaper, "is when this all happened. I mean, here we are every day, doing what we're doing, saying the same old things, and you . . . !" Kit blows her nose. "You make this, like, *mind*-blowing decision. And we don't even know!" I shake my head in disbelief.

"I'm sorry. . . ," Kit says.

"You're always *sorry*. . . ."

"Megan?" A warning note from Mia, standing in the doorway.

"You guys . . . ," says Elaine. I expect her to slap her hand down somewhere and call for a truce. "This isn't up to us to decide." She's looking right at me.

7

It feels good to be running again. It also feels terrible. My thighs jiggle, and I'm out of breath long before I should be. Usually I take off past Kit's and run as far as Elaine's and back, about three miles. This morning, I turn right and head toward what would have been my high school, away from the Clausens'. I don't want to think about Kit, not this morning, not until I absolutely have to. Last night I cried myself to sleep like a little kid. I don't know why. This morning I woke up knowing I needed to run. My soles hit the pavement, a familiar slapping sound, a good sound but a whole lot better when Spoof ran, too.

I don't like things to change. Sometimes I get angry about it, as if the world should stay still just for me. Does everybody feel this way, or is it just me?

I'm glad Mia has the breakfast shift. What will she say to Kit? Anything? And there I am thinking about Kit again. It's natural as breathing, which isn't very natural at the moment. Needles of ice are sticking in my chest.

Joe runs, really runs. I love to watch him at track meets, striding with his chest forward, legs pumping. He's beautiful as some wild animal then. *We're history.* The words really didn't hit me until later.

He hasn't called. And I don't call him—I don't know why. I guess that means we never went together, not *really*. Dad says the rules for calling guys are "archaic." A girl should be able to call anyone she wants to, anytime. I'm sure he's right. But somehow I just can't dial Joe's number.

"*We're history,*" he said. My history with men isn't exactly earthshaking, speaking of history. Donny "Turnip" Turner gave me a red cat collar to wear around my wrist in sixth grade (with bells on it!) and I got into this kissing thing with Mike Adderly—couldn't keep our lips off each other for about six months. That was in ninth grade. And then Joe off and on ever since. There's nobody I'd rather run with or see movies with or make out with. The rest, I'm not so sure about. Sometimes I feel left out of the loop, like the whole world is in on things I'm still guessing at. And now that Mia and Mando are finished, I don't know how much more I want to know. Things change. That's all you can count on. Not love, not promises, sometimes not even your friends.

I decide to run past Joe's. Maybe he'll look out his window. Maybe he'll see what he's missing. Maybe he won't notice that my thighs have turned to jelly.

I wonder what Mia's said to Kit. Mia can be awfully blunt.

School goes by in a long blur. I catch Mia between English and French. "Well?"

"What?"

"How was she?"

"Kit?"

"Of course Kit—who else?"

Mia is quiet for a minute. "There are other people in the world, you know, Megan."

At lunch, I stop at my house to pick up Kit's laundry. The Clausens' washer is the old wringer type. Kit says it nearly wrung the neck of some aunt of hers in 1968, so I'm giving it a wide berth.

Kit's laundry is folded neatly in a box stuck under my bed. I slide the box out, deciding that I'll be upbeat when I get to Kit's, no matter how I feel. I'll be wise and understanding. Noble. Compassionate. I won't say anything about the baby unless Kit talks about it first. I tell myself that it's none of my business. I decide that Mia's right. There are other people in the world besides Kit, besides Kit's baby. But it burns me that I didn't know what she was going to do. I think about all the things that Kit never told me, her supposed best friend. I thought she needed me. Now I just feel like the housekeeper. I grab the box of laundry and head on over to the Clausens'.

A jet black Lexus is parked in front of the house, but I figure whoever owns it is visiting people across the street. I prop the box of laundry on my shoulder and go in. Laughter floats down the stairs, a woman's high-pitched laugh followed by the deeper yuck-yuck-yuck of a man. I hesitate. Curiosity carries me up the stairs and down the hall to Kit's room.

The woman sitting on Kit's bed is maybe in her late

thirties. She has hair like a seal's fur—sleek, black, and short. Huge silver hoops hang from her earlobes. She's laughing, her head thrown back to look at the guy, who's laughing along with a little more effort. They stop abruptly when I come into the room, and the woman's eyebrows go up. Her eyebrows are two little sideways commas. Kit is wearing the General's nightgown. Her face is the merriest I've probably ever seen it. I feel like I've stumbled into The Comedy Club. "Hi, Meg!" Kit says. "What's in the box? Pizza?" She giggles; the woman chuckles; the man yuck-yucks. I set the box of laundry on her dresser. "This is Mr. and Mrs. Keefe—"

"Oh, *puleeze*, Kit! Lindsay and Jonathan." I shake Lindsay's hand and get poked with what feels like the Hope diamond. Jonathan Keefe, leaning against Kit's closet door, wipes the air with a wave. "Howdy," he says. He has a face like Mr. Ed.

"Lindsay and Jonathan," Kit says, looking from one to the other, "are the ones who are, you know, going to adopt the baby." Kit's cheeks are flushed. There are open boxes from The Limited on her bed, tissue paper, three or four sweaters and some other stuff. Matching socks. "Megan always comes by for lunch," Kit says, making me sound like a freeloader instead of the one who makes the sandwiches.

"How sweet," Lindsay Keefe says. "Would you like to join us, Megan? Jon's going to run out and get us a little something from the deli. Aren't you, darling?"

I start into my usual babble. "No, thanks. No, I was just going to make us some—no, that's all right. I was just going. . . ."

I feel squeezed out the door, like a zit.

*　*　*

In sixth-period Bio, I poke around the insides of Marilyn, Elaine's and my frog, while Elaine takes notes. "They don't *look* like parents," I say, having caught Elaine up on lunch at Kit's.

"You'll pardon me if I say that's a dumb comment." Elaine has new glasses, round with copper-colored wire rims. They make her look older, like a real scientist, which is what she hopes to be. Her perm's calmed down a little. The General says that Elaine will come into her own, as far as beauty goes. Elaine would rather be beautiful now. Later she'll be famous or rich, maybe both, and then she won't care about being beautiful. "What do *real* parents look like?" she says. "Your mother? She looks like a cheerleader. Mine?"

"You know what I mean." Marilyn is full of little yellow globs and long red and blue strings. "They're, I don't know, jet-setters or something. You should see her ring."

"Wealth doesn't exactly disqualify one from being a good parent, Megan." She frowns at me over the top of her new glasses. "I don't know why you and Mia are being so hard on Kit, anyway. She's doing what she thinks is best for the baby. You have to admire that."

"I do. Sort of. I don't know. How can she do it, Elaine? Could you? Could you just give up your baby?"

Elaine sets her notebook down. She looks troubled. "I don't know, Megan. I hope I never have to know. I just don't think it's our place to judge."

"Well, I can't help it. I'm trying, but all I can think of is that poor little thing swimming around inside Kit, thinking nothing's ever going to change."

"Girls? Is there something I can help you with?" Ms.

Sato is the soul of civility. Never raises her voice. Elaine snaps to attention. I poke my bug sticker into one of Marilyn's yellow globs.

Teen Sex (DRAFT), p. 2

J. L., a Taylor senior, says he's had unprotected sex with "two or three girls" in the last year. "Well, they don't say anything, and I figure, hey, they're on the Pill." When asked about his concern about sexually transmitted diseases and AIDS, J. L. shrugs. "Hey, I'm careful. These girls are, you know, clean and all. . . ."

S. R., a junior, says she carries a condom in her purse. "It's been in there for about two years," she says. "The same one. If you tell a guy you've got a condom, he thinks you're a slut!"

C. T., a freshman, says she's had sex only once. "But it didn't count because he pulled out in time."

L. L. doesn't want to hurt her boyfriend's feelings. . . .

The General is in the kitchen when I get home from school. She's got her NURSES DO IT WITH PATIENTS coffee cup in one hand. The other hand is on the counter, fingernails rat-tat-tatting the tile.

"Mr. Worfley called," she says, green eyes glittering. "That's your history teacher, in case you don't remember."

I try for casual. "What did he say?"

"Megan Lane, you know very well what he said!" *Clonk* goes her cup on the counter. I jump. "Since when do you cut class?"

"Is he sure it was me? I mean, he doesn't really know who we are. . . ."

She shakes her head. Inside she's burning. You can almost see the smoke. "I want the truth, Megan, and I want it now. Have you been cutting your history class or haven't you?"

In the silence the refrigerator hums. "Yes." I swallow hard. Mercy is all I can hope for. "Once." The General's eyes narrow menacingly. "Twice. Honest. Just twice."

Spoof pads into the kitchen, looks up at me with his sad retriever eyes. His tail thumps against the wall, and he pushes his cold, wet nose into my palm.

"Oh, Megan." The General sighs, as if her fire's suddenly fizzled. "I never thought we'd have to worry about school. Other things maybe, but not school. Why did you cut? Don't tell me—I know. Joe. Am I right? It's always boys."

I nod. What can I do? It's either that or tell her I've been lying to her longer than she knows, that I've been seeing Kit every single day, even though she's asked me not to.

"Of course you know you're grounded." She rinses her cup in the sink and sets it upside down on a dish towel. "No after-school activities, no going to Elaine's every night, no overnights with friends, and no dates. Absolutely no dates. One month."

"A month?" Spoofus collapses on the kitchen floor and lays his head on his paw.

"You heard me."

This won't work. Mia and Elaine can't take care of Kit without me.

"You spend entirely too much time at Elaine's anyway. I expect Elaine's family is getting tired of having another child around—"

"I'm not a child."

"Adults keep their word, Megan."

"What's that got to do with anything?" I follow the General out of the kitchen. She collects her purse and car keys on her way to the door. "And, besides, that isn't true. What about Nixon? What about Marie Antoinette—"

"Neither of whom lives here," she finishes for me.

I follow her out to her car. "So when haven't I kept my word at school?"

"Going to class is keeping your word," she says primly.

"Since when?"

"Since you entered a contract on the first day of school with Mr. Worfley. And with us"—she turns at the car door to face me—"your parents."

"You sound just like Dad. I didn't sign any contract—I know that."

"We make lots of agreements we don't sign, Megan. That's what being an adult means."

This gives one pause, as Dad likes to say.

But if contracts are what count, I want to say but of course can't, then I've made one big fat contract with Kit. And with Mia and Elaine. What do you do when your contracts overlap? Is there any way to win this one, or do I lose either way? If I honor my agreement with Worfley and my parents, I let Kit, Mia, and Elaine down. The reverse is also true.

If only Kit had thought things through before she went behind the barn (or wherever she went) with Monk. Were they making a contract when they did it? Isn't making love (or whatever you want to call it) a contract? And what kind of a contract does Kit have with her baby? Can she wipe that out and make one with the Keefes? It's all too much for me.

The General says I'm to talk with Dad about cutting class, as if that's something to worry about. We all know who makes the rules. What could be worse than a month in jail?

At 5:40, I pop two chicken dinners into the micro and wait for Dad. When his car scrunches up the drive, I punch the start button. He doesn't call my name from the door, so I know he's been briefed by the General. He comes into the den, drops his work on the desk. I've got his news channel on the TV and a drink already poured. He likes this really expensive scotch watered down almost to nothing. "Hi, Megan," he says, and drops into his chair. "That was one hellish long day." Eyes closed, he massages the bridge of his nose.

"Can I tell you my side of things," I say right away to get it over with, "before you decide if I should be grounded or not?"

Dad opens his eyes. He punches the off button on the remote and turns to face me in the next recliner. Dad looks like a lawyer. Even when he's in his pj's, he's got this lawyer stare that makes you want to confess, even if you didn't do whatever you were charged with, which in this case of course I did. "Shoot," he says.

"First of all," I say, mimicking as best I can all the *LA Law* reruns, "I admit that I cut class twice. And I promise that, in exchange for an amended sentence, I will not repeat the aforementioned crime again."

"I think we've already been through the penalty phase of this case," he says. "Go on."

"I want the record to reflect that I did not forge a note to excuse myself, which is what everybody else does—"

"Which is, as you must know, beside the point. Go on."

"Oh, Daddy," I say, crumbling, throwing myself on the mercy of the court. "I had to do it."

"Had to. As in forced? As in gun to your head?" There's a glint in Dad's eye, like he's enjoying this a little too much for my taste.

"Well, not exactly forced. It's just that if I didn't take Mia's place, Kit would get out of bed and maybe, well, maybe she'd lose the baby—"

There, it's out.

"Baby? Megan, what are we talking about here?" Dad was about to sip his drink. He sets it down.

And so I go through the whole thing, from Kit's October announcement at the Coffee Cat to today's lunch. Dad runs his hand several times over his head. "Why didn't you tell us?" he says finally. "I know that your mother doesn't want you to spend time with Kit, but this—this is, well, I just don't know—"

"Extenuating circumstances?" I say hopefully.

"I'd rather not have words put in my mouth, thank you, counselor." Dad squints, thinking. "Is Kit really that important to you?"

I nod.

"I thought you said she'd changed."

"She has! But that doesn't mean she's not our friend anymore, does it? We promised . . ."

Dad waits for me to finish, but I just can't say "friends till the end." It sounds so eighth-grade. "Well, I don't think your mother was aware of the depth of your friendship with Kit. I know I wasn't. Megan, we're not exactly made of iron, your mother and I. We bend."

"You, maybe."

"Look, I'll talk to your mother if you'd like. Explain what happened."

"No! No, Daddy. It'll just make her furious that I've been lying to her all this time. Just give me a week, okay? Let me keep doing what I've been doing—"

"You mean going over to Kit's when you said you were going to Elaine's." Dad frowns.

"Just for a week. I'll figure something out so that Kit gets what she needs. Then you can ground me. Please!"

He sighs through his nose. "A week," he says.

"Oh, Daddy," I cry, and throw my arms around him. "You're so understanding."

"A sucker, you mean."

"No way!"

For some reason my Hungry Man chicken tastes a lot better than it ever has before. I think maybe it's relief, not only that I've got a reprieve but that I'm finally sharing this thing with someone older than sixteen.

Elaine says she needs a new look to go with her new glasses. In her room she shows me the article in this month's *Glamour*. All you need, it says, is Five Basic Pieces. With the Five Basic Pieces, you can get Twenty Great Outfits. This is always harder than it looks. You go through your closet looking for something to start with, black slacks, a white sweater—everybody's got those, right?—but still it's hard to get "the look." If you want the Twenty Great Outfits, the article hints, you won't find them in your closet.

So far in Elaine's closet, nothing's even close. Elaine (over Mia's strenuous objections) has always gone the preppy route: cords, blouses with little round collars, pleated skirts, and pullover sweaters with sheep grazing on them. Naturally the Five Basic Pieces are simple and elegant, a long blouse in what they called silvery heather over which you're supposed to layer a short black vest or off-white mohair sweater. The rest is pretty much black. They call the collection an "investment," and you can see why when you check the prices in the small print.

I'm no help. Elaine just has me here for moral support. I'm the one dressed in jeans and sloppy sweatshirt, the one *Glamour* would put a black line through, the Don't! on the "Dos & Don'ts" page.

Downstairs our parents are playing ancient records on the stereo and dancing up a storm. It's the General and Dad's twenty-second anniversary, and the Caprittos are throwing them a party. Elaine and I are more or less baby-sitting. Soon after the party began, Elaine's brothers, who are permanently stuck in their nasty phase, were sent upstairs. Then Elaine's mother asked if we'd take Granny to her room. She'd been dipping into the punch bowl and was starting to nod out.

"Well, here's a vest." Elaine emerges from the depths of her closet and checks the picture in *Glamour*. "But it sure doesn't look like that one!" Her vest is navy knit with buttons shaped like daisies. She plops onto the bed, knocking the magazine to the floor. "I give up."

The door pops open, and Elaine's brothers stick their heads in. Their faces are painted in hideous stripes of puke green and black. They howl and dive into the room, race around waving their plastic weapons, leap on the bed and off. "Get out of here! Get out of here, you little creeps!" Elaine cries. They waggle their pointy pink tongues and race off down the hall. "God, I can't wait until I can leave this house!" She locks her door and falls back down on the bed. "Another whole year, plus what's left of this one."

"Yeah." Truthfully, I don't think much about what happens next. Change happens next. There's nothing you can do about it. Here in Elaine's room, I feel as comfortable as I do in my own. And it hasn't changed a bit.

Elaine continues in her dreamy voice. "My own place, at least my own dorm room. *Our* own room. . . ."

My Diet Coke pops open with a little explosion. I catch the foam with my tongue so it won't drip onto Elaine's patchwork quilt. Granny made it, and Elaine intends to take it wherever she goes. "What if we don't get into the same college? You'll probably get a scholarship to Stanford or Princeton. No way they're going to take me."

"Don't be so sure. Your grades are fine. And anyway, I'll just go where you go—that's easy enough."

"You'd turn down Stanford? Are you nuts?"

"Friends Till the End," she says with a grin. We share a high five. Her banner's identical to mine and to Mia's and Kit's. The difference is that Elaine's award certificates are tacked up next to hers, all in a neat row.

If Stanford calls, you listen. We both know that. Talk about change! But I don't want to think about it. All I change is the subject. "So you liked the Keefes?" Lindsay and Jonathan Keefe have just about moved in with Kit. They're there whenever I go over, or at least Lindsay is. Mia and Elaine report the same thing, only they don't seem as upset about it.

"Well, he's kind of a dork," Elaine says reluctantly, "but she's okay. A little hyper, but that's probably because she's so excited about the baby. They tried everything— drugs, operations, having sex every which way. You should hear the story—it's fascinating."

"I'll bet." Lindsay and Jonathan Keefe engaged in kinky sexual practices isn't my idea of fascinating.

"What bothers me a little, though, is the way they shower Kit with stuff. It's too—I don't know . . . *obvious.*"

"What stuff?"

"Clothes mostly. A pair of leather boots to die for, that real soft expensive leather. Now they're talking a car."

"I didn't see any boots."

"Well, Kit knows the way you feel. . . ."

I push myself up against the headboard and cross my arms. "Well, do *you* think it's right? She's getting bought off, Elaine!"

Elaine rolls over to face me. "That's one way to look at it," she says.

"And of course you have another." Secretly I've always admired Elaine's ability to balance things, to see both sides. She's a lot like my dad that way.

Elaine shrugs. "She's had a rotten life—what can I say? These people are like *her* parents, you know? Kit's been wearing our hand-me-downs forever—well, *yours*." Elaine laughs. Even Kit at her hardest up wouldn't go preppy. "Do you really think she needs to be, well . . . *noble*? Would that make it all better?"

I guzzle my Coke. "What do I know? I just think the whole thing stinks. I just think she's going to be sorry someday, that she's going to want the baby back and that Mrs. Lindsay Keefe will forget she ever knew her."

Elaine sits up, cuddling her pillow. "Yeah, that could happen. What also could happen is that the baby gets a life and drives a Lexus to her classes at Stanford."

"So? That doesn't mean she'll be loved."

"It doesn't mean she won't be, either."

Three sharp thumps against the wall, and our thoughts are derailed. Granny.

Granny's room is a whole other world, lamps with glass shades and fringe, doilies, ancient photographs, a rug

Granny braided when she was a young girl. No television. Granny reads. If she's not reading, she's listening to talk radio. She's on a first-name basis with all the hosts. She calls them daily, two or three times if it's a religious topic. "I thought you'd be asleep," Elaine says.

"How can a body sleep with all that racket going on? You'd think they'd be too old for that kind of nonsense." Granny's frail, spotted hands tremble on the arms of her rocker.

"Do you feel like eating something now? They've got some great stuff down there." Elaine's as worried about losing Granny as I am about losing Spoofus. I suppose that kind of comparison is a little tacky. Only a true dog lover could relate.

Granny says she'll have a little something, but nothing "deviled."

Downstairs things are in full swing. Beatles, Rolling Stones, and Dad's favorite, Vanilla Fudge. The living room is a sea of bobbing heads and waving arms. Elaine rolls her eyes. I imitate Mrs. Jackson doing the twist. Elaine cracks up. In the Caprittos' kitchen, the food's still covered up or in the fridge, but we figure since it's Granny, we can take what we want, so we load up.

Granny's nodding off again by the time we get to her room, but Elaine wakes her up. "Pâté," Elaine says, handing Granny her plate. "Your favorite."

"What's that?"

"Pâté. Liver."

"Liver mush?"

"Well, sure. More or less." Granny looks tempted. She hunkers down over her plate.

Elaine and I settle ourselves on the floor. I've loaded my plate with a little of everything except the General's taco salad, which she makes just about every week on one of her days off. The General's more into convenience than taste.

"What's this, then?" says Granny before she tries each thing. Elaine patiently tells her, describing in detail what everything is made of. I can tell she's ad-libbing so that Granny magically gets all her favorites.

"What's that they're celebrating down there, anyway?" Granny says between bites. "A wedding?"

Elaine tells her.

"Twenty-two years, huh?" Granny studies me, the daughter, and her old eyes sharpen. "You married yet?"

Elaine and I whoop. "No!" I cry. "I'm only sixteen."

"Old enough," Granny says. "Wait much longer, and you won't get the pick of the litter."

"Gran!" Elaine looks genuinely shocked.

"And don't make the mistake Elaine's aunt Dolores made, either," she says, poking her fork in my direction. "Don't give it away."

"Give what away?" I ask innocently, barely able to keep from breaking up.

Granny leans forward, sticking out her wobbly chin with its two long white hairs. "You know very well, young lady. And you know right where I'll be when they hang out *your* sheet!"

"Oh, Gran," Elaine sighs, "they don't do that anymore. That was in Italy, years and years ago." She turns to me. "Can you imagine? The whole town would gather under the bride's window the morning after to see if the sheet had blood on it."

"Well, that's the problem with the world now, isn't it?" says Granny. "A gal can lose her virginity and nobody knows. Nobody sees the evidence. What's to keep her from giving it away?"

"Well, you don't have to worry about me, Gran. I haven't had a date since the ninth-grade Sadie Hawkins dance."

She's conveniently forgotten the blind date Joe and I set her up with. I guess it was worse than we thought.

"That's a good girl," Granny says. "Now I'm going to read my Bible for a little while and get ready for bed. That party just about wore me out."

"Well, that's one approach," I say, laughing, when we're back in Elaine's room. "The old bloody sheet." But Elaine's not laughing. "Hey? You really buy that stuff?"

"God, no," Elaine says. "It's just that—"

"What?"

Elaine sits on her desk. She picks up a pencil and twirls it slowly through her fingers. "In January? Remember? When there was that family wedding in Sacramento? Dad's second cousin's daughter, or whatever she was?"

"Yeah?"

Elaine's eyes behind the new glasses look wider, more dramatic. "Well, something happened."

"What happened?" It's funny how life seems to stand still just before you hear something that changes it forever.

"Let's just say there wouldn't be a bloody sheet for me." Elaine bites her lip. She's halfway between cracking up and tears—I can't tell which.

"No!"

"Shhhh! I was going to tell you before, but there was all this stuff with Kit and—"

"Elaine! Who was it? What happened?" My mind is racing ahead. That makes me last. That makes *me* the only one. I don't know why that matters, but it does.

"Well, it feels so stupid now, but, well, when I was growing up and we lived in Pittsburgh?" Pulling her knees up, Elaine wraps her arms around them.

"Yeah?"

"My cousin Greg lived with us for a while. His mother got remarried or something, and the new husband didn't want Greg. Well, he and I, well, we fooled around a lot, you know, like kids do. . . ."

I can hardly put into words what I'm thinking. "You're not saying you did it with your cousin?"

"Fourth cousin," Elaine says. "It doesn't even count."

"*Right*, doesn't count."

"It was like this . . . experiment, Meg," she says earnestly.

"Right, *experiment*." I don't sound like a friend, I sound like a snotty twelve-year-old. It's just that I'm so knocked out.

"No, really. That's why I did it—I don't know about him. He says he'd always had this crush. But me? I just had to find out for myself what it was like."

"And?"

"And I found out that it's something you do not do as an experiment." She gives me a rueful smile.

"Were you, you know, careful?"

"Now, what do you think? Come on, Megan. You're talking to Madame Curie here. You've seen me in lab." She studies my face. "You're mad, aren't you? You think I'm a slut, right? Or you want to use me in your article. *What?*"

"The *s*-word never crossed my mind, dummy." I'm

remembering all the little hints Elaine's been throwing out, things I haven't caught because of Kit, because Kit and only Kit's been on my mind. "I'm just . . . I don't know. Surprised. We were going to wait."

Elaine looks sad. It was her idea in the first place to make that promise. "I've let you down," she says.

"Not really," I try to explain, dropping into her bean-bag chair. "At least not the way you think. It's just that . . . that nobody tells me *anything*."

"That's not true, Megan. Kit tells you stuff she doesn't tell anybody else—you know that. She told about Monk, for one thing. And who did Mia call when Mando broke up with her?"

"Only because she couldn't make it to Kit's."

"I tried a couple of times to tell you—"

"I know you did."

"So, forgive me?"

"Of course, dummy."

"We all talk to you, Meg. Sometimes it's a little hard to jump right in"—she watches my face—"because"—she hesitates for a second—"because sometimes you come off a little like your mom."

"Like the General?" My heart plummets—anybody but the General.

"Hey, it's not such a bad thing," Elaine says, sliding off the desk. "Your mom's great. That's the problem. She's kind of, well, perfect. The rest of us make mistakes."

"And I don't?"

"Get real. Of course you do. I'm not saying *you're* perfect!"

"That's a relief!"

Elaine laughs. "Thanks."

"For what?"

"I don't know," she says, suddenly shy. "For all kinds of things. For not judging me. For being my friend."

"Friends Till the End," I say. We pretend we can bring eighth grade back, just like that, but we know we're kidding ourselves.

"But could I . . . I mean, do you mind if . . . ?" I'll be a great reporter someday, Elaine says, because I can never let a story go.

"Sure," she says, "as long as you don't use my name or anything like my name. Call me Gertrude."

"But there isn't a Gertrude in the entire school."

"Well, there should be. What's a high school anyway without a single Gertrude?"

"Okay, Gertrude," I say, pretending to scribble in my notepad. "Exactly why did you decide to have intercourse?"

"I told you," she says. "It was an experiment."

"Like the atom bomb."

"More or less."

"And what did you think of your experiment when it was over?"

"I thought, Now, that was really stupid."

"Did you, Elaine?"

"Gertrude. Yeah, I thought it was really stupid."

The party starts to wind down a little after midnight. The oldies are slow-dancing now. Elaine's dropped off to sleep in her clothes. I'm sitting on the steps, watching Dad and the General dancing to "Blue Moon." Her head is resting on his chest. She has the sweetest most un-General-like smile on her face. But it's his face that gets me. His head is bent so that he's looking down at her, and on his face is a look of such tenderness that it brings a lump to my throat. Twenty-two years, I think, twenty-two years and they still feel like that. Maybe I won't ever get married—who knows? Maybe I'll never have sex. But if I do, that's the way it's going to be. If I have to wait half my life, it's going to be just like that. Otherwise, why bother?

One day left of the week that Dad's promised me. Elaine says she'll take over at Kit's as much as she can, Mia will double her checkup calls from work, but I'll have to keep sneaking out between the time Dad's gone to sleep and the General gets home.

And then there's Lindsay Keefe. But is she there to take care of Kit or just to make sure she gets the baby?

After school, I interview the members of the Chastity Club, all girls.

"And how many members do you have?" I ask.

"Just us."

"The four of you?"

"That's right. But it's a real club," the president says. "We have a charter and a pledge and everything."

"And what do you do? Fund-raisers? Car washes? What's the club for?"

They look blankly at each other. Then the president

says, "It isn't what we *do*. It's what we *don't* do." The other three girls smile in agreement.

"Did you ask them about their belts?" Mia says later on our way to my interview with Liz Grant about Citizens for Responsible Schools. Mrs. Grant lives in the kind of neighborhood where you can't see the houses from the street.

"Huh?" I'm busy looking for house numbers, which nobody seems to have.

"Their chastity belts." Mia couldn't get over the Chastity Club. Was there a Fallen Angels Club? If not, should she start one? "Maybe there's some new kind now, without padlocks."

"This is one intimidating neighborhood, Mia. I was pretty confident about all this till we got here."

"Don't worry—you'll do fine. Here it is, 6780 right?" She pulls up to a massive iron gate and a call box. We give our names, and the gate slowly swings open.

"I know what you should ask her," Mia says, as the old Barracuda follows a winding driveway lined with hundreds of bright orange birds-of-paradise. They gaze scornfully down their pointy beaks as we pass. "You should ask if she's willing to adopt all the babies that get born because of her campaign."

"Do not say a word, Mia. Not one word."

"Don't worry. I'll just chew on my tongue. But how could somebody like this understand Kit's life, for example?"

"Kit didn't use any birth control, remember?"

"Yeah, well, maybe she would have if condoms were dispensed in the girls' room like tampons."

"May I quote you in the article?"

"Damn straight you can!"

The entrance turns out to be the most impressive thing about the house. Not that the house isn't fabulous. It is, but in an understated way. Kind of long and rambling, sand-colored adobe with an ancient red-tile roof. It looks like a house in which normal people might live.

Liz Grant greets us at the door. No butler. She's wearing jeans, just like a regular person. "Why don't we go out on the back patio?" she says. "It's such a lovely day. Can I get you a Coke or some iced tea?"

The "back patio" faces a gorgeous rolling green carpet that goes on forever into the distance. I thought it might be a golf course, but it's only the Grants' "back lawn."

"So," Liz Grant says. "At last we get to talk." She plops onto a lounge chair. "I suppose you want to know all about CRS, how it came to be, what we believe in, that kind of thing." She slides open a wooden box and takes out a cigarette. "You don't smoke, do you? Oh, tell me you don't!"

"Well . . . ," Mia says. Liz Grant passes Mia the opened box. They light up, foreheads scrunched.

"Okay," I say, punching the record button. "What is it that you believe?"

"It's simple," Liz Grant says. "No sex, no babies!" She waits, and when we don't laugh, she laughs for us. "I'm kidding, girls. I only wish it were that easy. But that's really the bottom line, isn't it? If we could convince young women to wait out their teens at least, we wouldn't have unwanted babies, out-of-wedlock births—"

"Why just young women?" Mia says.

"Mia," I warn. "Mrs. Grant—"

"Liz," she says.

"Liz. What exactly is the position of CRS on birth control? Is it just condom dispensing that you're against?"

"That's our current campaign, yes. Condom dispensing is like saying"—she stops to find the right phrase—"like saying, 'Have at it, kids!' "

Mia's chewing on her tongue—I can tell.

"And you believe that without condoms kids wouldn't be as likely to have sex—is that it?"

"We just don't believe it's an issue for schools to take on. Would you like another Coke? Cookies?"

Mia can't keep still—I should have known. "But if schools won't deal with it, who will? Parents?"

"Yes, parents. Of course. CRS is founded on parental rights. Sanctity of the family."

"Your family maybe," Mia says, catching my scowl. "Well, I'm sorry, Megan, but all families aren't like the ones in this neighborhood." She turns her attention back to Liz. "Some kids never see their parents. Not because their parents don't want to see them, but because they're working. Two jobs, in some cases. There are kids with terrible parents, drug addicts, criminals. Kids without fathers. Kids without any parents at all. I just don't see how you can leave this thing up to parents, not in this day and age."

Liz looks thoughtful, concerned. "There is a problem, of course," she says. "A terrible problem. But that's just it, you see. Condom distribution just adds to it. So a child uses a condom one time. Who's to say he'll use one the next time?"

"But we'd want him to, wouldn't we?" I've forgotten all my carefully composed interview questions and am going with my gut instinct, a journalism no-no. "At least he'd be protected from disease. And so would the girl he was with."

Liz sighs. "There is no guaranteed protection," she says, "not from disease. Not from getting pregnant. It's a false promise. I'll tell you something," she says, then hesitates as if she might be changing her mind. She glances at my recorder. "Off the record." I punch the off button. "Our daughter came to us when she was just fourteen . . . *fourteen*. She was pregnant, she said. Wouldn't say who it was or how it happened. We were distraught. Here was this . . . honor student! This bright, happy—or so we thought—child. This child! Well, our religion forbids abortion, which would have been terrible in any case. She went away, just like in the old days, to a home. And she gave our—she gave the baby away. Do you know I still think about that baby? Every day of my life. I wonder if she or he is well cared for. If she's happy. We could have given a grandchild so much. . . ."

I say that I'm sorry. Mia is still caught up in the story, taking both parts, the daughter's and the mother's. She's on the verge of tears. Liz comes back from a long way off and seems almost surprised that we're still here. "Well, clearly we didn't know our own daughter."

"It happens. I mean, not to be rude, but it isn't just bad girls who get themselves pregnant. It can happen to anyone. I'm sure you did your best, but kids do what they do. Some are just experimenting." I shrug. Liz looks horrified. "Sure, if we could get everybody to just say no, that would solve a lot of problems. But can we?"

"We have to try," Liz says, shaking off her sadness. "Handing out condoms is giving our permission—it's as simple as that."

A great reporter would ask it, but I can't. A great

reporter would ask if Liz's daughter wouldn't have been better off carrying a condom in the pocket of her jeans. On the record.

"Well," Liz says, slapping her thighs. She's back to her old confident self, and I can tell she's given us all the time she wants to give. "Do you have enough?"

"Sure," I say. "I guess."

"Say hello to your mother, Megan," she says at the door. "She and I have gone round and round on this thing at school board meetings. CRS never misses a meeting!"

"Who's her daughter?" Mia says when we're in the car again. "She must be our age."

"I dunno. Private school, I guess."

"Oh, of course. Should have guessed."

"I was thinking about Kit the whole time, weren't you?"

"Sure. How could I not?"

"Not quite the same, is it?"

"Isn't it? What's the difference?"

Mia turns out of the private drive and heads toward school.

"You didn't exactly chew your tongue," I remind her.

"I couldn't help it. Especially when she said that stuff about young women! Why should it all be up to us? Liz couldn't even get her own daughter to say no—what a crock!"

"Mia?"

"Yeah?"

"Do you think there might be something—I don't know—something wrong with me?"

"Sure, lots of things!" Mia laughs until she sees that I'm serious.

"I really like Joe, you know? But when it gets close to . . . *that*, I back right off. It's not even a problem. I mean, I *want* to. But then I don't. Does that make sense?"

"Makes sense to me. You're not in love—that's all."

"But even if I was, Mia. Is it worth the hassle? Really? Be honest."

"Talk about loaded questions! You sure know how to ask them. Is it worth it? Yes. Yes and no. Yes, it's wonderful. When it's right. When you're ready. And, no, it's not worth the risk. What can I say?"

"Thanks," I say. "I think."

Teen Sex (DRAFT), p. 3

In the past ten years, there have been two unsuccessful attempts to institute a sex education course at Taylor. The first was an after-school "club" initiated by a concerned teacher who was transferred out of the district the following year. The second, sponsored by Planned Parenthood, would have provided condoms free of charge to any student who asked for them, as well as birth control devices (with parental permission) such as cervical caps and IUDs. "Sure, they can buy their own rubbers," Ms. Adams says. "But they don't. If I had youngsters, I'd try to protect them any way I could. Good healthful food, vitamins, and, yes, today it would be condoms." Both programs were dropped within the first two weeks because "a handful of nutsy parents" protested, according to Ms. Adams.

But will condoms protect you from AIDS? Although they are "substantially safer"-when used with a spermicide-according to Ms. Adams, for all age groups, condoms have a 10% failure rate.

H. T., a sophomore, doesn't have an STD, nor does she have AIDS. She knows because she's been tested. What H. T. has is a six-month-old baby. "My mom watches him while I'm in school," she says. "But she's gotta go back to work. I can bring him to the YMAS center, I guess, but I'm thinking maybe of dropping out. You know, just for now. Then I could work, too." The father of the baby wasn't mentioned.

It's Tuesday, the General's night off, and I've decided to cook dinner. This pleases Dad and worries the General, who would just as soon make another taco salad and avoid the mess. It's true I use a lot of pots. I figure all great chefs do. Tonight's dinner is going to be chicken cacciatore, Elaine's mom's recipe with lots of garlic and extra-virgin olive oil. I figure I'm the only one allowed to use it now. I get the oil sputtering hot and lay in the chicken pieces. "I wish you'd clean up as you go," the General says, tossing the plastic chicken tray in the trash.

"Leave it!" I cry. "Don't touch a thing. I'll clean it all up—I promise."

The General breaks down. She smiles. "Okay," she says. "Call me if you need me." Fat chance. Literally. If the General made chicken cacciatore, it wouldn't have a speck of oil. And it would taste like stewed cardboard.

Being grounded isn't as bad as I expected. Not that I'm about to admit it. Our house, even if it is a little too neat, is a real home. Like Elaine's but completely unlike poor Kit's. Mia's place is a different story altogether. She and her aunt live in an ultramodern condo with bare wood floors and huge uncovered windows. There's art—and not just prints, either—everywhere. It's gorgeous, but you can't find a comfortable place to settle in.

Being grounded kind of puts things in perspective. It wasn't my idea, of course, and there's nothing I can do about it. It's like someone (the General, in this case!) reminding me that I'm not the one in charge of the world. It's a bit of a surprise but one I can live with.

The problem, I realize as I flip the sizzling chicken pieces, is that I still worry about Kit, even more when I'm not there. It's as if I can keep something awful from happening, even if I know I probably can't.

While the cacciatore simmers, I set the table with the good dishes. I almost set one for Danny. Still. That's another change I'm never going to get used to: Danny at

Berkeley. He hardly ever calls. The General says that's normal, but I can tell she misses him a lot. You can hear it in her voice when she calls him, every Friday the minute Dad gets home.

The phone rings in the den. "It's Joe," Mom says, handing me the cordless. She gives me a look. Poor Joe. She thinks it's all his fault.

"I've been thinking," Joe says. He sounds so serious that I avoid the usual sarcastic comeback. "I've been thinking that we should go to the prom."

"We should? As in you and me?" My blood pressure goes straight up the scale. "I thought we were history."

"Aw, I was just messing around. Thought I could change your mind."

"Joe?"

"Yeah?"

"My mind's not going to change. If you knew me better, if you knew what's been going on, you'd know that."

"Hey," he says, "I didn't call to argue. Really. I, well, I kind of miss you, you know?"

"Yeah, I miss you, too."

"I don't have fun with anybody else, at least not any other girl."

"Well, at least you've been trying. *That's* good."

He ignores my sarcasm. "So what about the prom?"

"Sure," I say. "As long as I can wear my jeans."

"Up to you," he says, and I almost think he means it. "And maybe we could, you know, like see a movie sometime."

"For fun," I say.

"For fun, Megan," he says. "For fun."

The dinner's great. The General's surprised. Dad eats seconds, which he never does. "You know, I think you've got the feel for it," the General says.

"Don't put ideas into her head," Dad warns. "*After* med school, she can go to culinary school if she wants to."

Med school? Is he serious?

I tell them that Joe's asked me to the prom. The General actually looks pleased. She worries that I'm permanently bonded to jeans and sloppy sweaters, Danny's old plaid flannel shirts and baggy gray sweats. I tell her I have to be loved for what's *inside*. How can she argue with that?

"Agatha's Attic has some lovely dresses," the General says, already envisioning me in something I probably wouldn't wear to my own funeral.

"He asked me to a movie, too."

The General's back on full alert. "But of course you told him you're grounded. The prom's in May. That's different."

"I'll forget what Joe looks like by then."

"All the more romantic," Dad says. I kick him under the table.

At ten I make a great show of total exhaustion and head on up to bed. I read a chapter of *Pride and Prejudice*, one ear listening for the sound of my parents turning in. I wait what seems like forever. I call Kit and tell her I'm coming over.

"About time," she says.

"What?"

"Only kidding."

I get there a little after eleven. Kit's awake, a pile of glossy-looking brochures scattered across her lap. She quickly gathers them up. The brochures show flashy new cars from different angles, going up the sides of mountains, sliding around hairpin turns. I look at one. A woman with startlingly blond hair and pale skinny arms whips a Mustang through its paces. It's Barbie. It's always Barbie. I decide to keep my mouth shut. As Elaine says, it's Kit's life. I'm beginning to wonder if keeping your mouth shut is a big part of being friends till the end.

I slide into bed next to Kit. "So? How's it going?"

"Awful."

I check her face to see if she's serious.

"I mean it. I feel like a blimp, and I get these pains—"

"Where? Is it labor?"

"Unh-uh. My chest. It's hard to breathe sometimes."

"Did you tell your doctor?"

"No, not yet. Well, Lindsay gave me some stuff she said wouldn't hurt the baby. It's just gas, she says."

"Lindsay? She's not a doctor, Kit. I think you should call your doctor."

"Sure, okay, I will." She punches the remote. Some guy on David Letterman is sucking whipped cream out of a dog's mouth. End of conversation.

Kit falls asleep with her head against my shoulder.

Mia catches up with me after first period. "Did you hear?" Her normally honey-colored face is pale.

"What?"

"Come here," she says. "Come over here. I don't want anybody else to hear, though it's probably too late. . . ."

I follow Mia to the teachers' parking lot. One glance at teachers' cars and you can see how much they don't make. It doesn't seem fair, and I'd probably do something about it if I were in charge of the world. Meanwhile, maybe Dad's right—med school's not a bad idea.

"Now, this could be just a rumor," Mia says. "God, I hope it is!"

"Tell me!"

She hesitates; then she blurts it out: "Monk's HIV."

"HIV? You mean HIV-positive? Monk?"

Mia nods solemnly.

My mind tries to compute as my eyes watch the stream of kids passing, just kids, normal kids, kids like us. I know Monk. Monk taught me how to skate.

"Supposedly he went to this bachelor's party last year, somebody he knew from L.A., and there was this girl everybody did it with. Well, almost everybody. The guy who's spreading the rumor didn't do it." Mia grimaces. "Nice guy."

"But what about Kit? Oh, Mia! And what about the baby?"

"Exactly."

We stand there looking at each other, not knowing what to say and certainly not what to do. The bell rings for third period.

"I'll tell her," I say.

"We all three will," Mia says. "You tell Elaine. See you at the Coffee Cat."

Teen Sex (DRAFT), p. 4

Whose fault is it that kids are getting AIDS? Opinions at Taylor

range from "queers" to "sluts."
It's hard to find even one student
with a real understanding of the
disease and how it is transmitted,
yet according to statistics by the
year 2001, 1 in (Megan, check this:
?) students will be diagnosed HIV-
positive. "Girls don't get AIDS,"
says G. R., a sophomore. "It's a
guy thing." L. L., a senior, does
use condoms so he "won't get stuck
with a kid to support." He believes
condoms will protect him "absolutely" from AIDS as well. He says
he's "pretty sure" his girlfriend
isn't HIV-positive, but she hasn't
been tested and neither has he.

The Coffee Cat is jammed. Our booth's been taken over
by an Aspiring Writer camping out with her Powerbook.
It doesn't look like she's going anywhere anytime soon.
Mia takes this on as a personal campaign. We need that
booth. We have things to take care of, lives to fix. Mia
lights a cigarette and leans over the side of the booth like
a vulture, her cigarette not a foot from the lady's ear.

"Mia . . . ," Elaine warns, but Mia ignores her.

The woman shifts in her seat. She looks up at the
cigarette. "Oh! Sorry," Mia says, but in a few minutes
the cigarette's back where it was. The woman closes her
Powerbook with a little click. She gathers up her books
and jacket. She gives us a nasty look, but who can blame
her?

"So we tell her," Mia says. "What then?"

Elaine brings us coffee and scoots into the booth. "This is so terrible," she says. "I can't stand to think about it."

"Yeah, well," Mia says, the old tough Mia, "you have to. Not thinking about it is the whole damned problem, it seems to me. But what I'm wondering is, what if he doesn't have it? What if it's really just a rumor? I think we need to find out for sure, before we upset Kit."

Nothing will go down, not even coffee. I stir in packets of sugar, fill it to the brim with milk, anything to occupy my mind.

"She should have an AIDS test anyway," Mia says.

"We could—I don't know—not tell her," Elaine suggests. "Just make sure she gets tested."

We think the scenario through. Kit won't hear about Monk because she's not at school, not unless he were to tell her himself. I mention the possibility.

"Monk?" Mia's eyebrows go straight up. "You see him around here? At school? He has the good grace to at least be embarrassed, if not completely terrified. He's not talking."

Elaine slides a cigarette out of Mia's pack and sticks it between her lips. She's done this before, just to get a laugh. This time she strikes a match, squints, and lights up. I can't believe my eyes. "Elaine!"

She coughs, waves the smoke out of her face. Her eyes tear up behind the new glasses.

"Don't tell me," I say. "It's just an experiment, right?"

"Oh, give me a break, Megan," she says, and stubs out the cigarette.

Carrie Starnes comes in with a couple of her friends,

leans over, and whispers dramatically, "Have you guys heard?"

"Carrie," Mia says. "Grow up."

We gather our stuff and take off. The Coffee Cat has lost its appeal, at least for the day. We pile into the Barracuda and drive around. Nobody says much. After a while, Mia pulls into the East Beach parking lot. We get out and shuffle through the dry, heavy sand toward the water. It's low tide. Dogs everywhere. There's a leash law, but nobody pays any attention to it. There's a dog that looks just like Spoof when he was a puppy. He splashes through the surf after a tennis ball but can't quite get his mouth around it.

We walk in the wet, hard-packed sand toward the wharf. "I vote for telling her," I say after a while.

No response.

"I mean, it's her life, right? Besides, I think we should stop trying to protect her from things. She's got to grow up." I almost add, "Because she's going to be a mother." But then I remember she won't be a mother for long.

"Meg's right," Elaine says. "I vote to tell her."

"But you guys!" Mia insists. "What if it's not true?"

"How can we find out?" Elaine says.

"Ask Monk," Mia and I say at the same time.

Elaine stops. We turn to face her. "Well," Mia says. "Got any other suggestions?"

"I'm not going to ask him," Elaine says. "I don't even know him."

"Well, I do," Mia says. "And so do you, Meg. Or at least you used to."

"In fourth grade! Our parents hung out. . . ."

"Well . . . ?"

We walk a little farther, thinking. A wave sneaks up on me, soaks my shoes. I'm thinking about Monk, about how one minute somebody can seem like a waste of skin and the next day be just a person. I slip off my shoes, tie them together, and hang them around my neck. Kit thinks I expect people to be perfect, but she's wrong. Even Dad, who's about as close as people get, isn't perfect.

"We'll ask him together, Meg," Mia decides.

My shoes knock against my chest. I'm remembering how much fun it was to skate with Monk. And then I remember what Kit said. "We can't tell him about the baby, Mia."

"We won't," she says.

When we get to his house, Monk's polishing the wheels of his prized Mustang, each spoke with the loving attention the General gives Great-grandmother's silver. He looks up, surprised, then wary. Monk's the kind of guy who will always look like he did when he was ten. The crew cut helps. "What's up?" he says.

"You want the long version or the short version?" Mia says.

Monk frowns. "The short one."

"We know about you and Kit."

Monk looks almost relieved. "So?"

"So we're worried."

Monk glances at me. "Still skating?" he says.

"I could probably skate the pants off you," I say. If I could just bite my tongue off. But Monk either doesn't make the connection or lets it slide. He buffs his fingernails, avoiding Mia's eyes.

"It's all over school, you know," Mia says.

He looks up, and I see right then that it's no rumor. My heart hurts, like it's been punched. "Yeah, I know," he says.

"Is it true?" Mia isn't being her tough self now. She's always liked Monk. She even said once that if it weren't for Mando, she might be interested.

"'Fraid so," he says, and tries a grin. It doesn't quite work.

"Damn!" Mia says. "And you weren't going to tell anybody?"

"Hey," he says. "I am telling. I just didn't tell Kit yet."

"Why not?"

"Her old lady," he says. "She scares the hell out of me."

"We'll tell her," I say. "If she doesn't have it, then maybe the ba—"

"Meg!" Mia covers her own mouth, as if she was the one who slipped.

"The *what*?" Monk looks like the wind's been knocked out of him.

"Baby," I say miserably. "She didn't want you to know."

"Oh, jeez!" Monk says, throwing up his arms. "What else can happen?"

"To you, right? To you!" I think Mia's going to slap him, she's so angry. "It's your fault! If you'd kept your fly zipped when you should have, none of this would've happened!"

"Mia," I say quietly, leading her away. "Come on. Leave it."

Monk watches us drive away, his ten-year-old face aging by the minute.

10

I can't sleep. A full white moon floats in the right-hand corner of my window, and my whole room looks like a movie before it's been colorized, black-and-white, shades of gray. I close my eyes, and I'm skating for the first time alongside Monk; I open them and we're not eight anymore. I try to hate him, but I can't. Just like I can't stay mad at Kit for long, or judge Elaine, or fault Mia for throwing stones from inside her own glass house. Things really aren't black-and-white when it comes to people.

I crawl down to the end of the bed and lay my head on Spoof's fat tummy. He breathes like he's been smoking a pack a day for the last ten years. He lifts his sleepy head to check me out, then drops it back down. He needs a bath. In the morning, I'll smell just like him. My head swims toward sleep.

* * *

The Lexus is parked in front of Kit's when the three of us arrive in the Barracuda. "Well, we'll just tell her to leave," Mia says. "Who does she think she is anyway?"

I remind Mia, in case she's forgotten: "She thinks she's the mother of the baby."

"Not yet, she isn't." Mia stomps up the walk; Elaine and I follow.

Lindsay and Kit are perusing college catalogs. "Some of these places!" Lindsay exclaims. "What I wouldn't give to be seventeen again!" Lindsay's wearing inmate stripes—black-and-white baggy top and stretch pants. The outfit has a logo I don't recognize, probably something Italian.

Kit doesn't look good. Her skin is pasty, the shadows under her eyes deeper than ever. I think maybe we shouldn't tell her about Monk, not now. Or that we should get her to a doctor and then tell her.

"Lindsay thinks the schools back East are better," Kit says. "But I said I'd only go where you guys go."

"Great!" Elaine says. Mia and I exchange glances. We've been trying to interest Kit in college practically since the first day of the poetry project, and *now* she wants to go?

"Look at this brochure," Lindsay says, like it's show-and-tell time. "Davidson. It's in North Carolina. Gorgeous campus. 'Princeton of the South,' they say here."

"Mrs. Keefe."

She looks up. "Lindsay," she insists.

"Lindsay. Do you mind if we talk with Kit privately for a while?" I sound nearly as reasonable and mature as I intended. Mia looks impressed. "Of course," Lindsay Keefe says, but I can tell she's a little put out. "I only came by to bring the catalogs. Jon and I will stop and get something at Russo's for dinner, sweetie," she says, leaning over to kiss Kit on the forehead. Mia and I say the things with our eyes Lindsay Keefe wouldn't want to hear.

We listen for the door to close downstairs. We wait for the Lexus to purr away into the distance. Kit looks at the three of us looking at her. "What? You think I'm a creep, right? I can go to college, you guys! I couldn't even think about it before." I climb into my place on the bed beside Kit. Mia and Elaine sit on either side. Kit gets increasingly nervous. "What? You think I should change my mind about the baby, right? You think I should keep the baby." Tears well up in her eyes.

"Kit, it's not that," I say.

"Yeah? Then what?"

"There's this . . . problem."

Kit checks Mia's face, then Elaine's. She looks back at me. I almost can't go on. A good wind could knock her flat. "Tell her," Mia says.

"It's Monk," I say.

"You told him!"

This is a detour I didn't expect. "Well, kind of, yeah. I mean, I didn't intend to but—"

"Megan! You promised!" Kit sits up. Her arms flail around her fat middle, groping for pillows. Elaine leaps to the rescue, propping pillows behind Kit's back. Kit leans back with a sigh. She closes her eyes. "What did he say?"

"It's worse than that," Mia says.

Kit opens her eyes.

"Monk's HIV-positive." I'm amazed I can spell out the letters.

Kit goes into her freeze zone. Not an eyelash quivers.

"So you've got to get tested," Elaine says. "Right away. Maybe everything's fine. But if it isn't . . ."

Kit's hands reach around her belly and rest there on top. She comes out of her freeze slowly, like she's making a great effort. "I think I'm going to be sick," she says. Mia leaps up; I go for the wastebasket, dump it, and set it down under Kit's bent head. Up comes whatever she had for lunch. I brace her forehead like the General does. Elaine brings a wet washrag from the bathroom. Mia looks a little green. Kit heaves and heaves.

"Do me a favor," she says to me when she's through. She wipes her blotched face with the washrag.

"Sure."

"Call Lindsay," she says. "Here's the number. Tell her—I don't know. Tell her something. I don't want anybody around right now, just you guys."

"Okay," I say. "What about Shirley?"

"I'll tell Shirley," she says, sounding braver than I know she feels. "Oh, God, you guys, am I going to die? What about the baby?" She starts to cry, big choking sobs like I've never heard before. Elaine cradles Kit like Shirley might have done once. I hold her hand. Mia pats her leg. We're a mess, but we're there.

I wake up with a great title: "Teen Sex: Get It While It's Hot. Or Not." At school I find some more kids to interview. A senior says, "Most girls are just asking for it, if you ask me. Look at what they wear!" Another boy quotes a long passage from the Bible. A girl advises "sticking with girls because it's safer." I corral one of the young moms in the child-care center. "Well, if I didn't get pregnant," she says, diapering a wriggling infant, "I wouldn't have her! She's the best thing that ever happened to me!" I want to ask the baby if that goes both ways, but she's just too young.

I spend the rest of the afternoon finishing up the story. Kit's made an appointment with her doctor, Elaine says. Mia will take her in on Tuesday.

I'm running the spell check when Abe, the *Trib*'s editor in chief, bursts in. "You should see what's going on out front! All hell's broken loose!"

I grab a notepad and race after him. The front lawn is crowded with dozens of people. They spill out onto the sidewalk to where the KEXT News crew is unloading cameras and cable. Kathy Kincaid ("This is Kathy Kincaid, Channel 6 News. Have a safe one!") wades into the crowd. "Excuse me!" she yells, waving the mike over her head. "Excuse me! KEXT, Channel 6! Excuse me!"

The Wart is fending her off with his hands and retreating. "Turn that thing off!" His face is dark red. The collar of his white dress shirt is damp with sweat.

Somewhere just behind the hub of the crowd comes the chant. "*AIDS off campus! AIDS off campus!*" I recognize those voices. Liz Grant gives me a curt smile and resumes her chant: "*AIDS off campus!*"

"What's this all about?"

Abe shrugs. "Beats me." Kathy Kincaid and Mr. Wartner battle their way toward the Admin building.

"Mr. Wartner, please," Kathy Kincaid cries, pushing the mike in the Wart's red face. "Just a few words. What's your position on the boy with AIDS?"

A voice in the crowd yells, "It isn't a boy—it's the football coach!"

"Nobody has AIDS!" yells the Wart. "Turn that damned thing off or I'll break it!"

"Then why the protest?" Kathy says.

"They're misinformed," the Wart yells over the excited voices of the crowd. "It's all blown out of proportion."

"What's blown out of proportion?" says Kathy into her mike.

"If you don't leave right now," the Wart says, standing his ground, "right now, I'm calling the police. You're on school property." He begins backing Kathy and her crew down the lawn toward their van. Kathy is rapid-firing questions the whole time. "Are you going to expel the boy? Are there others? Is it the coach? And what about your condom distribution program?"

"Once and for all, we do not have a condom distribution program! Look," the Wart says, having gotten the upper hand, "back off for a while. Let this thing simmer down a little. Then ..."

"You'll talk?"

"I'll talk," the Wart says, looking like he'd rather face a firing squad. "I'll say a few words."

Abe and I hang around until CRS winds down to a croak and the crowd has mostly wandered off. Wart spouts the usual garbage to the camera, in other words nothing, but it sounds important. Kathy leaves looking a little deflated but still game. You get the feeling she could pop right out of that van anywhere, anytime, with two minutes' notice. If you're a reporter, you have to admire that.

"Turns out you've got the hot story," Abe says back in the Trib room. "When's it going to bed?"

"So to speak."

"Ah, but appropriate."

We're both blushing and pretending not to.

"I'm finished." I click the mouse on PRINT and wait for hard copy. "You can have it in five minutes."

"Nice work, Megan," he says genuinely. "You're really getting a name around here. Keep it up and you'll have *my* job." He lifts "Teen Sex: Get It While It's Hot. Or Not." from the printer. "Great title!" He's reading as he heads for the cubicle that's his office. I tingle all over. Not that I'd ever want his job. I have bigger things in mind. Stories nobody's heard, features never written. The truth about high school that never gets told. "Oh, yeah, Megan broke that story," they'll say someday. "Went on to win a Pulitzer just a year after high school graduation."

Danny's due any minute. He's surprised the General by deciding to come home instead of skiing at Tahoe for the weekend. You'd have thought she won the lottery. But I'm looking forward to seeing Danny, too. We're not your usual, or should I say normal, brother and sister. We don't fight. We never called each other horrendous names or wished we were only children. We actually played together when we were younger, or we did until he hit middle school, when I became more or less invisible. Then sometime during his sophomore year, Danny woke up again and realized I wasn't too bad. That I could even be an asset, particularly if I had friends who looked like Mia. And Kit was nuts about him. All this with Kit would have been easier if Danny'd been home.

Around here if you put a turkey in the oven and it isn't a holiday, it's got to be some special occasion. The General of course does everything by the book, Betty Crocker in this case. If Betty says a half teaspoon of this or that, the General doesn't deviate by a flake or a grain. Like a lab tech, she measures in the appropriate amount and levels it off with a butter knife. So what you get is your supertraditional turkey dinner. The exact same dinner you could get at Mel's, the old folks' cafeteria. The exact same dinner you had last year, and the year before that, back to the year you first ate solid food.

I suggest sour cream for the mashed potatoes, a little nutmeg in the carrots. "Well, perhaps next time," she says, holding a measuring cup up to the light to make sure the milk isn't an illegal fraction of an inch above the half-cup line.

I'm setting the table with two extra plates when Danny comes bursting through the door. That's how he is. Other people enter; Danny bursts, his green eyes flashing. "The conquering hero returns!" he says. "Bring me mead! Bring me women!"

The General grabs him. They hug, rocking back and forth.

Danny grabs me next, scratching my face against the rough collar of his Cal jacket. "Hey, kiddo," he says, "I missed you." How many brothers would say that? He smells like the remains of a Big Mac and fries. I hang on to him until he finally lets me go. He and Dad do the sort of hug and dance that men do when they can't bring themselves to do the real thing, patting each other's backs, saying manly things:

"How was the drive?"

"Oh, not too bad. . . ."

Even Spoof comes down the stairs to welcome Danny home, standing patiently by Danny's side until he's noticed, tail swaying back and forth. "Aw, Spoof," Danny says, kneeling. He roughs Spoof's head just the way Spoof likes it. "Old Spoofus, old guy." Spoof makes that funny sound, half bark, half whine, as if he wants to say something really bad but just can't get it out. I lift Danny's duffel bag to carry up to his room. "I invited Mia over for dinner," I say nonchalantly. "Hope that's all right."

"All right with me," he says. I can't tell whether he's pleased or doesn't care one way or the other. Maybe he's got a girl at Berkeley. A couple of them, an honor student for during the week and a party girl for the weekend, though I have to admit that doesn't sound much like Danny.

What's not so good is that I haven't told Mia that Danny's home, that this isn't just your ordinary everyday dinner with the folks. She'll see right through me. She'll know that I'm trying to fix them up. But Mando's moved on, so what's the difference? Elaine saw him at the movies with another girl—no one we know, but she had, Elaine said, one of those "aristocratic" faces. That was my chance to get back at Elaine. "As in long nose? As in elegant long neck? As in horse?" Elaine agreed that you couldn't exactly tell the rich from the rest of us just on looks alone, but it worried us both just the same. It confirmed how tied Mando is to his mother. He wasn't coming back to Mia, and she might as well get on with things. That's when the wheels began to turn.

I'm stirring flour and water, perfectly measured, into the roasting pan and thinking that if the General would get out of my way, I'd slip in a little brandy. The doorbell rings. "Let Danny get it," I tell her. And then I can't help myself—I have to see exactly how the two of them act, what their eyes say, the minute he opens the door. That's all I need to know. No sparks and I drop the whole thing.

But Dad goes to the door. I asked Mia to wear the stretchy black dress she wore to Kit's shower. The General said she'd buy me one, I lied, but she had to see exactly what it looked like first. Mia doesn't mind if somebody else has the same dress. Why should she? Next to her I'd look like a flagpole painted black. She comes into the kitchen without having seen Danny, or vice versa. "That's quite a dress," the General says with a little lift of the eyebrows.

Mia takes that as the compliment it might have been. "Oh, thanks!" she says. "I really think you should get one for Meg. It wasn't expensive."

The General looks at me as if to ask, What's going on? I return the same look: *Beats me!* Mia turns, releasing something into the air that smells like an evening in the tropics (as if I know). And there's Danny, stopped in the doorway, his mouth open like he's about to say something but can't think what that something might have been. His eyes are on Mia, but she's at the sink with her back to him. That, of course, is enough. Mia's hair falls softly to her waist. It glows in the light of the lamp that hangs over the kitchen table. The dress, on the other hand, is about as short as a dress can be and still qualify. From there on down, her legs go forever, long and curved, the color of dark honey. She hates her feet because they're so big, but from the back you can't tell that. Besides, who looks at feet?

Mia turns. She sees Danny, and her eyes, already wide, open just a little more. They say, what? Surprise? Interest?

"Hi, Mia," Danny says.

"Hi, Danny," Mia says.

Hardly memorable lines for the start of a big romance,

but neither of them seems to be able to move or say anything else. "Here," I offer, handing Mia the gravy spoon. "Stir this."

But Danny's still in a trance. "Tell your father dinner's ready," the General says. She hasn't missed a thing. There's a half-smile on her face as she glances from Danny to Mia.

"Who's saying grace?" Dad says as we take our seats. "Megan, how about you?"

"I will," says Mia. We bow our heads and join hands, Mia's slim dark one joined with Danny's. Mia's prayer is in Hawaiian, a kind of chant with lots of vowels and long words starting with *K*. I sneak a peek at Danny, who looks properly enchanted.

"That was lovely," the General says after we've all said amen.

"She speaks Japanese, too."

Mia's eyes say I can shut up anytime.

All this gives Dad a chance to tell one of his few jokes. "What do you call someone who, like Mia here, speaks three languages?"

Nobody bites. Finally Mia, looking around the table to see why no one's answered, says tentatively, "Trilingual?"

"Absolutely correct," Dad says. "And what do you call someone who speaks two languages?"

"Gee, that must be bilingual," I say dryly.

"And what do you call someone who speaks one language?"

Again, no bites. Finally Dad can't wait. "American!" he says.

We chuckle just to please him. "That's almost not funny," the General says. "We should all be speaking Spanish, at least here in California."

"Danny and I took Spanish," I remind her.

"*Si*," Danny agrees. "And a lot of good it did me. I took the exam at Berkeley and I'm back in Spanish I. *Está muy estúpido!*" He smiles at Mia, who gazes back sympathetically.

We pass the peas and carrots, the bowl of ordinary mashed potatoes, the canned cranberry (indented with the ridges from the can). Dad carves. He's picked up the charged mood in the room, but you can tell he doesn't know where it's come from. "I know you like the breast," he says to Danny. "And what about you, Mia? Leg? Thigh?" Mia doesn't dare look at me. "Anything's fine," she says. Dad plunks a leg on her plate and adds a little breast meat, just to make sure.

Dad and Danny offer to clean up after dinner. Mom, Mia, and I "retire" to the den. "I'm whipped," the General says, flopping back in her recliner.

"Would it be all right," I begin, "I mean since Danny's here and all—"

"Megan, you're grounded. It doesn't make any difference who's here. Being grounded is like, well, penance or something. It gives you the opportunity for reflection, not diversion."

Mia looks decidedly uncomfortable. She hardly knows what "grounded" is. "I'll go help with the dishes," she says.

"What about Mia and Danny?" I ask when Mia's gone.

"Mmmm," the General says, "cute."

"They'd probably like to go out somewhere later, but I think they'd be a little uncomfortable without—"

"Megan, you're grounded."

"Yes, ma'am."

I just happen to still be up when Danny comes back. "Have fun?"

"Nope," he says with a dramatic sigh. "She's a drag."

"Danny, be serious!"

"Speaking of serious, you didn't tell me you've been grounded," Danny says. Danny and I polish off the last of the pumpkin pie, huge slices slathered with vanilla ice cream. "What's going on?"

So I catch him up on Kit. "And she's going to give the baby up," I say as we each dig into a second piece.

"For real?" he says, his blue eyes troubled.

"For real," I say.

I can see that his mind is going back over earlier times with Kit, when he was her big brother almost as much as he was mine. "Well, she's only sixteen," he says. "I guess it's the smart thing to do."

"I guess. . . ."

Danny looks at me, changes what he was about to say. He's let his sandy blond hair grow longer. He looks a little scruffy, but still cute. Older, too. "What if they don't want the baby, after all," Danny says, "these people Kit found?"

"Are you kidding?" I say. "Lindsay Keefe is stuck to Kit like a coat of paint."

"Does she know Kit's been exposed?"

"No."

"The plot thickens," Danny says.

I carry our dishes to the sink. "So what about Mia?" I say nonchalantly, watching milky water swirl into the drain.

"Yeah," Danny says.

"Yeah?" I turn and look at him. "What's yeah?"

"Just *yeah*. She's great. What did you expect? But isn't she tied up? Like in almost married?" He stands up and stretches nearly to the ceiling.

"It's over. Mando told her she should be free to have fun her senior year."

"Well, he's right," Danny says. "I'd do the same if it was me."

Terrific.

All's quiet on the school front Monday morning. Just before the lunch bell rings in the *Trib* room, I get a yellow office summons, my first real one. It's even signed by the Wart and not his administrative aide. Abe's eyebrows go up, but I take it in stride. My courage probably has something to do with the fact that I haven't done anything wrong. I sure haven't cut class. I pass a couple of girls hanging a banner announcing the junior prom.

The Wart is out of his office, talking with his aide. "Ah, Megan," he says. "Come in. You can go ahead to lunch, Mrs. Beamis. We'll let voice mail get the phones."

I follow the Wart into his inner sanctum. One look and you can see why he's a principal. He never left high school. Baseball trophies line the walls, pictures of the Wart's younger self, a shock of dark brown hair falling in his face. He's about forty pounds lighter and surprisingly cute. Tom Cruise in a baseball uniform. My respect goes up a notch. I take the seat in front of his desk. He walks to the window and stands with his back to me. My recorder as always is in my pocket. I think about pushing the record button but decide I'd better not.

"Well, of course, you're aware of"—he separates the

blinds and peers out, then looks over his shoulder at me—
"the trouble we've been having lately."

"Sure." I decide to record this after all.

"It's giving Taylor an awful image. Just terrible!" He
leaves the window and drops into his swivel seat. He leans
back, rubs his chin, and sighs. His hair has been cut in
perfect half-circles over his ears. "We need to lay low,
Megan," he says, like we're great friends, like we go way
back. I'm surprised he even knows my name. "We need
to let this thing blow over."

"Yes, sir."

"Your article . . ."

"My article?" I start to make some connections.

"For the *Trib*," he says. "Good writing, by the way.
But not exactly . . . appropriate, if you know what I mean."
He smiles like a dentist with bad news.

"You read my article? Already?"

"Of course. I read everything that goes in the *Taylor
Tribune*. It all has to be approved."

"Well, but—" I think twice about reminding him of
all the times the paper went out without his approval.

"This is a high school, Megan, not the real world." Is
he serious? He is. "You can't talk about . . . about young
people having . . . relations. You can't use words like . . .
well, like, *sex* in a school paper! It's even in the title! We'd
have the school board down our throats, not to mention
that bunch of mothers. . . ." He glances toward the window, probably remembering his fifteen minutes of
unhappy TV fame. "By the way, isn't your mother on
the school board?"

I nod.

"Well?"

"She hasn't read it."

"Ah!"

"But she'd want to see it in print—I know she would!"

"Maybe. Because it's her daughter. But I'm sure she'd see the bigger picture."

"What is the bigger picture, War—Mr. Wartner. If you don't mind my asking."

He doesn't hesitate for a second. "Reputation, Megan, reputation." And then I realize he's right. The General *would* agree with him. Absolutely.

"So it just goes down the tubes?" I stand up, face flaming, ears ringing.

"The story?" Did he think I meant the school? "Well, young lady," he says with a paternal chuckle. He swirls me around and guides me expertly toward the door. "I'm sure there are lots of stories around here for you to tackle. Taylor has more Merit Scholars this year than any school in southern California—did you know that? And what about the foreign exchange program? Now, *there's* something worthy of your time! Give my best to your mother." I'm suddenly outside the door, which closes behind me with a solid click.

Mrs. Beamis leafs through the Wart's appointment book. The date pages slip through her fingers like the opening of an old movie and spill away. "Look," Abe says, "we just need to see the rule, or whatever it is. The code. The law that says we can't print what we want to without his approval. Maybe you could get it for us."

Mrs. Beamis has a truly astounding collection of cat's-eye glasses. This pair is pearl-studded pink with matching pearl leashes. She doesn't answer, just keeps leafing.

"Or maybe we could get a copy from the superintendent."

She looks up, appraises Abe, maybe knows his father's the district attorney. Her pearls clatter. "Perhaps Mr. Wartner can see you at lunch," she says. "On Thursday."

"We're wasting our time here," Abe says as we leave the Admin building. "Let's just deal with the superintendent." It's good sharing this thing with Abe. Before my story, he didn't seem to remember who I was from one time to the next. Which is reasonable, considering that he's a senior.

"I thought he was in Bali or somewhere."

"Tahiti. You're right. Some kind of educational conference. Yeah, right!"

I say what's been sitting on the tip of my tongue. "Why don't we just run it?"

"Run it? As in run the article anyway?" Behind the thick lenses of his Buddy Holly glasses, Abe's brown eyes widen. I know it's a minority opinion, but brains can really be cute.

I shrug. "What's the worst that could happen?"

Abe and I have a lot in common. We're Capricorns, his parents are still together, his dad's an attorney, his mom does even more committees than the General, he's got an older sister at Berkeley, but above and beyond all that is his almost completely submerged desire to blow the lid off things.

"We could get suspended. Kicked out. Expelled." Words meant for other kids, "bad" kids, not Megan Lane, not Abe Klipstein.

"For telling the truth? Abe, all we're doing is saying how it is. How it really is."

The bell rings. Kids stream out of classroom doors and head in all directions, equations and grammar drills dropped behind like candy wrappers drifting to the lawn. Would they even read my article? Would it make a difference?

"They don't want to hear how it really is."

"You mean the Wart." Abe and I wind our way through milling kids toward Biology.

"I mean They. The big THEY. The solid brick wall of administrators, teachers, parents. Scares 'em. It's easier to play ostrich."

I stop at the door to Ms. Sato's class. "Forget what I said."

"You mean about running it?"

"Yeah."

"Cold feet?"

"Maybe." And just maybe, I'm thinking, the way to deal with a wall is to walk right around it.

At our station, Elaine's gotten Marilyn pinned in her usual undignified position. Elaine's new glasses have slid down her nose. She squints up at me, quickly evaluates my frenzied state of mind. "What's going on, Megan?"

"War," I say.

"Where?"

"In the real world."

"Where?"

"On campus."

"Oh," she says, poking Marilyn. "I thought you said the real world."

"To what or whom do I owe the pleasure of your company?" Dad says as I hand him his drink. "Or have I misspoken? Why the long face?"

"Nothing." I open the oven and check the status of our Superdeluxe Gourmet frozen pizza. "The Keefes are taking Kit her dinner, Thai food. Like she really needs it! We can't get them to back off." I pull the pizza out of the oven and slide it onto the cutting board.

Dad's forehead squinches with fatherly concern. "Megan?"

"Can't I just have a long face? After all, I'm grounded. Isn't that enough?"

"Is it Kit? Come on—you can tell your old dad."

"Couldn't you just, you know, bring a *real* pizza home sometimes? This stuff sucks." Tears prickle my eyes.

"Megan?"

"Okay, okay! It isn't Kit, at least not at the moment. It's the *Trib*. I just need to know if freedom of the press applies to high schools."

Dad doesn't answer right away. Running the cutting wheel through the pizza seems to require all his attention. "Hmmm," he says when the last slice is free. "Interesting. My first impulse is to say, it certainly should. Why, what's up?"

"My article got pulled. The one I've been working on for weeks."

"Ah!" he says. "The one about . . . what was it? Teen-age sexual practices. Wasn't that it?"

" 'Teen Sex: Get It While It's Hot. Or Not.' Well, I guess it's not."

"Too hot for the administration, I suppose."

In the den Dad flicks on the TV.

"What would happen if we ran it anyway?"

Dad gets sucked right into Peter Jennings.

"You're not listening."

"Yes, I am."

"Then, what? What if we ran the article anyway? What could happen?"

"Well, I don't know," he says, leaning back in his chair, wiping pizza sauce off his chin. "I seem to recall a case having to do with this some years back. Some high school in Colorado. Don't know how it settled. I could look it up.

But meanwhile," he says, "meanwhile, I don't think you should run it."

"Kit's been exposed, Dad." The words just say themselves somehow.

"Exposed?"

"To AIDS, Dad. She's getting tested tomorrow."

Dad clears his throat, a signal that he doesn't particularly like what he's about to say. "Look, Megan," he says. "I want Mom to know what's going on here."

"No!" Actually I'm not as surprised as I sound. "You promised."

"I know I did," Dad says, caught, as he likes to say, "between a rock and a hard place." "I won't tell her. But I want you to."

"Fat chance."

"I'm serious, Megan. I want you to do this."

"She'll kill me."

"She'll be upset that you've gone against her wishes, yes, but I think you need her, Megan. So does Kit."

At ten to ten, Dad is out cold in his chair. Spoof's asleep at my feet. I tiptoe out of the room. Neither of them stirs. It's still pretty early for me, but I'm suddenly knocked out. Too tired to go over to Kit's. I look at the telephone thinking, Maybe, just this once, I could call instead. I lift the receiver, but I can't dial Kit's number. Instead I grab a jacket from the hall closet, which turns out to be Dad's windbreaker. In the pocket are a couple of golf tees and thirty-five cents.

It's a dark night. Streetlights cast leaf shadows on the sidewalk as I pass the old oak tree, yawning.

Kit's house is dark. She's forgotten to leave the porch light on. I trip going through the front door, grope around inside for the wall switch.

"Kit?"

No answer. I call again, "Kit?"

I find the switch, and the shadowed foyer half emerges in dingy yellow light. The house is bone-chilling cold— it always is no matter the temperature outside. The stairs wind up into darkness. I call the cats, hear the strangely disembodied sound of my own voice. Minky slinks out of the dark hole of the living room and weaves through my ankles. I cradle her against my chest. Halfway up the stairs, footsteps echoing, I call Kit's name again. The TV answers with canned laughter. I pass Shirley's room through flickering television light.

Kit's on her back, her stomach huge and distorted, a bent arm across her eyes. I pull up the covers, carefully so as not to wake her. "Megan?" It's almost a whisper. Kit's arm drops back, and she tries to raise her head.

"Hi, kiddo. You okay?"

"Help me," she says weakly. "Help me up." She holds out a hand, and I grab it. I brace her back as she attempts to sit up.

Kit's hand is too cold. Her forehead is covered with sweat. "Kit? Kit, I'm going to call the doctor."

"No, wait," she says, clutching my hand. She sits statue-still on the edge of the bed, her head hanging. "I've just got to—" She falls forward suddenly, half into my arms, half onto the floor. I stumble under her weight. We end up together on the floor. We could laugh at this. "Kit?" Only it's real; it isn't funny.

"Kit!" She doesn't answer. She's heavy in a way that scares me, heavy like a heap of damp towels. "Kit!" I grab her chin and turn her face toward me. Her eyes are closed, her mouth slack and open. "Oh, God, Kit!" I wriggle out from under her, lay her down as carefully as I can on the rug. I pull a blanket off the bed and cover her. I try to find a pulse. I hear myself crying, muttering, talking to Kit, but it sounds like somebody else. I hear a woman talking—it's only the television. Kit doesn't move. I trip over Mr. Bear and grab the telephone. It clatters to the floor. I dial 911, hands shaking. I think about the 911 television show, how they always get there in time. I remember thinking I never wanted it to be me making that call.

Kit still hasn't moved. Is she even breathing? A woman answers. I try to say all the right things into the receiver, but my teeth stick together. The woman asks questions in a calm, everyday voice, but I can't remember the number on Kit's house. I panic. The number won't come. I know this number—I know it! Finally I tell the dispatcher it's seven houses to the right of 1637, my house. How can I forget the number on Kit's house? I've seen it a million times. It's nailed to the fence. Black letters, but I don't know what they are.

The dispatcher tells me to stay calm. She says a "team" is on its way. I picture football helmets, sweaty red jerseys. She tells me to check to see if Kit is breathing. She sounds like she does this a dozen times a night. I wonder if she has children. I crawl next to Kit with the telephone. I babble something into the receiver. Tears are streaming down over my hand onto Kit's shoulder. I can see a tiny pulse beating in Kit's neck, but her face looks blue. I tell the dispatcher that she's breathing but that she doesn't look good. "Kit?" I brush Kit's hair back from her face. Is she just asleep? Maybe she's just asleep. "Wake up,

Kit." I lay the receiver down and put my arms around Kit's body, around Kit and her baby. I lay my head on her shoulder. I listen hard for a siren. I can hear the dispatcher's tiny voice faraway in the receiver, but I don't let go of Kit. After what seems like forever, I hear a siren. It screams as it nears Sycamore Street. I lie with Kit in my arms, watching the walls of her room turn red.

Nothing's slower than the fat black hands of a hospital clock. "It's been almost an hour, you guys. Forty-six minutes. What could they be doing?"

"Are you sure your mom would tell us?" Mia says. "I mean if something bad—"

Elaine stops her pacing and plunks down next to Mia on the couch. "Nothing bad's going to happen, Mia. I don't want to hear that. It's important for us to focus positive energy here." Here she goes again, Mia says with her eyes. "I'm serious, you guys. It has to do with this wave-particle theory stuff. Energy's as real as, well, that lamp." We all look at the lamp, which could easily win the World's Ugliest Lamp contest. "We can help Kit if we just concentrate our energy."

"You're over the edge, Elaine," Mia says. She gets up and crosses to the window, looks out into the parking lot, where cars wait in pools of yellow light. 1:36, the clock says.

The last time I waited in this room was when Danny broke his leg, about ten years ago. Nothing's changed since then. I guess I should be pleased about that. But it's such a depressing room, unless of course you're a *Brady Bunch* fan. It looks just about like their living room. Orange plastic couches, spindly-leg tables piled with last year's magazines. Even the plastic plants look like they'd rather be somewhere else.

The General said she'd tell us what's happening "as soon as there's anything to know." I know that's Medicalese for "Keep your britches on; we'll tell you what we think you should know when we think you should know it."

I can't stop shaking inside. Elaine's got an arm slung over my shoulders to help warm me up, and the General brought me a cup of hot tea loaded with sugar just the way I like it. Mia watches with sad, worried eyes, chewing on her thumbnail. "Kit's going to be all right," Elaine says. She's been saying it over and over like a chant.

"Up here!" I yelled. That's what I remember, the sound of my own voice finally coming out of me, loud and clear.

They were two guys in light blue uniforms and a woman who I thought was a guy because she had no hair. None. She wore about six earrings in each ear, but she was all business. Before one of the men could pull me away from Kit, she had a cuff wrapped around Kit's arm and was taking her blood pressure. She asked me Kit's name. "Kit!" she yelled, like a punch in the air. Kit's eyes fluttered. Then she reached into a metal toolbox for something wrapped in paper, and when I saw it was a syringe, reality clicked in. "She could be HIV-positive," I said. "Be careful." The bald-headed woman looked directly at me for the first time. I watched what passed wordlessly between her and the men, and the plastic gloves came out. Then everything seemed to happen at once. Kit was strapped onto the collapsed gurney, and as the two men lifted her, the woman listened through a stethoscope for the baby's heartbeat.

They let me climb into the back of the ambulance, or at least I think they did. I don't remember asking if it was all right. I held Kit's hand. It seemed to have no life in it. I sobbed and held her hand and said her name over and over. She was wearing her angel earrings, the ones Mia gave her for her fourteenth birthday, tiny gold angels to guard her. There was a plastic bubble over her nose and mouth attached to a hose, and I could see that she was breathing. I breathed along with her. I prayed that the baby was breathing with us. We sped through dark city streets without stopping once or even slowing down, except a little at intersections. There was no traffic. People were sleeping, safe in their beds, where they should be.

We screamed straight up to the Emergency entrance. The ambulance doors opened, and all three techs jumped out at once. They slid Kit out, locked down the gurney's wheels, and she was gone.

I stepped out onto the asphalt, and there was the General. Her eyes said so many things I couldn't read them all, and I didn't try. I didn't even wonder how she knew I'd be there. I just grabbed for her like somebody drowning and bawled my eyes out in her arms. When I heard her pager go off, I let her go. Her collar was sopped with my tears. "You need some hot tea," she said, patting my hand.

"I'll let you know the minute I know." She turned and headed off down the hall at a trot. They needed her for the baby—I knew that. I knew where she was going.

"Ma?"

She turned. "Yes?"

"Thanks." I think she knew what I meant or what I was trying to mean. It wasn't just that she was there, though that was part of it. It was more a blanket thanks that went all the way back to the minute I was born.

She frowned. "We have things to talk about, Megan."

I smiled. I couldn't help it. I almost laughed. Maybe it was hysteria, maybe I was out of it, but the General was back in command, and, at least right then, I wouldn't have had it any other way.

Elaine comes out of a trance in which she has been concentrating every bit of her waves and particles on Kit and the baby. "Do you think we should call them?"

I know who she means, but Mia doesn't. "Who?" she says.

"The Keefes," Elaine says. "I don't know. . . . Would Kit want us to?"

We exchange looks. We all say we don't know at about the same time. We drop it. 1:52. After a while Elaine says, "Well, *should* we?"

"Go ahead," Mia says with a weary sigh. "It's their baby, right? Besides, somebody's got to pick up the tab here."

"Mia!" Elaine cries, as if she's been personally offended.

"Well?" says Mia, her eyebrows raised. "The meter's

132

running. You think the hospital isn't counting every Band-Aid? Kit's mother can't handle it—that's for damned sure."

Elaine, face flushed and scowling, goes off down the hall to find a telephone.

"Mia?"

"Yeah?"

"She's not going to die, is she? I mean, she's not dead, right? Kit can't die!"

"Friends Till the End," Mia says softly, her eyes tearing up. Mia doesn't cry easily. I guess that's why I expect her to be such a rock, but she just keeps more inside. "Remember that? We didn't believe it could really end, though. We didn't think about . . . about things like this."

"I don't think Elaine could handle it," I say. I picture us at Kit's funeral, Mia dressed in her skinny black dress. I kick my mind back into the present. Kit isn't going to die. Why do I picture things like that? Elaine's right. We have to focus our energy. I close my eyes and realize I don't know how to focus my energy. So I say a prayer instead. And then I do this little apology thing because it isn't like I talked to God just yesterday or anything. He probably doesn't even remember who I am.

Elaine comes back. "They're on their way," she says. "Lindsay sounded—I don't know—kind of excited. That's awful, isn't it? I mean kind of . . . ghoulish."

"We shouldn't have called them," I decide—a day late and a dollar short, as Dad says. "Maybe Kit will change her mind." Nobody says *if* Kit *can* change her mind.

The General strides in and perches on the edge of the couch, her back straight as the truth. She looks like she just showed up for work—not a wrinkle, not a spiky eyelash out of place. "They took the baby," she says. I think at first she means the Keefes; then I realize she means that Kit's had a Caesarean. "A little girl. Almost five pounds."

"Oh!" cries Elaine. "We knew it would be a girl. And we didn't even pick a name!"

"And Kit?" Mia's been reading Mom's face for clues.

"Stable," Mom says. "She's in ICU." The General looks at me, and I know she's remembering, as I am, our last "talk," the time Kit's stomach got pumped. *Kit is a troubled young girl, Megan. She needs therapy. I know you want to help, but you can't. She leans on the three of you, and you're just . . . just girls! I can't make decisions for Elaine and Mia, but as for you . . .* It went on from there.

Elaine asks if we can see her.

The General looks from Elaine to Mia to me. "You're supposed to be eighteen, but I can probably get you in for a minute." She checks us over. Mia and Elaine look wiped. I can only imagine how I look in my raggiest gray sweats and Dad's windbreaker. "Are you sure you wouldn't rather go home and get some sleep? She's going to be here for a while, you know." Our faces give her the answer she expected all along. "Okay. Well, be patient. I'll see how she's doing."

"Ma?"

"Hmmm?"

"Is she . . . Does she have, you know . . ."

"We won't know for twenty-four hours," she says. "Try not to worry about it." She checks my face and frowns. "I'll be back in a bit, okay?"

Lindsay nearly runs head-on into the General at the door. "Oh, my God!" Lindsay cries, arms in the air. "We were *dead* asleep! Wouldn't you know it! What happened?" I catch myself wondering whether Lindsay sleeps in full makeup or if she actually took the time to do that three-toned job with the eyes before jumping in the car.

Jonathan Keefe has his hands stuffed way down into the pockets of his trench coat. "Who's the pediatrician?" he demands. I shrug. He looks like he'd just as soon step on me as ever look at me again. "Do they even have a decent pediatrician in this place? Lindsay!" She snaps to attention. It's the first time I've seen who really runs things. "Did you even think, even *think*, to line up a pediatrician?" He looks at the three of us girls in turn, as if we did something terribly wrong and he's just found out about it. "What the hell is wrong with Kit, anyway?" He turns back to Lindsay. "I thought you said she was a healthy young girl. And now . . . this!" He waves his hand in the air, searching for words to match his mood. Then he stomps out the door, looking for whoever's in charge.

"Kit's in ICU," Mia tells Lindsay.

"Huh?" says Lindsay as if she can't for a second remember who Kit is.

"It was her heart," Elaine says. "Something to do with her heart. Probably congenital or"—she looks down at the floor; Elaine hates half-truths and rarely gets caught telling them—"*something. . . .*"

"Oh," Lindsay says blankly. Then as fast as a blink, she pours on the old Lindsay charm. "I'm *so* relieved! You can't imagine how your call hit us!" She picks up a magazine, frowns at the cover, drops it back on the table. "Like bricks! Like a ton of bricks. Well," she says with a big smile, "well that's *good*, then. That's good she's doing well." She focuses for some reason on me, her eyes wide, the pupils tiny black dots. "And the baby?"

I say nothing.

"It's a girl," Elaine says quietly. "Five pounds."

"Oh!" Lindsay cries. "Five pounds! Why, that's not small. I thought, well . . . but five pounds!" She holds her face between her hands, fingers spread like the arms of a starfish. Above her dark red fingernails, her eyes dance excitedly. "Will they let us see her?"

"Kit?" I say, just to be mean. I know she doesn't mean Kit.

"Of course," she says, hardly skipping a beat. "Kit. The baby, too, of course!" Lindsay looks a bit loony, like she's taken a blow to the head.

"*Of course* Kit!" Mia and I say at the exact same time.

Jonathan Keefe comes barreling back, the tails of his trench coat flapping around his legs. "Won't tell me a thing. They've got the baby quarantined or some damned thing."

"Isolated," Lindsay says. "You mean isolated. Is she in one of those, you know, plastic things?"

I tell her it's called an isolette.

"She shouldn't need one of those, should she? Five pounds!" Lindsay says. "She shouldn't be in . . . one of those plastic things."

"Damned if I know," her husband says, pacing the length of the waiting room and back. He runs his hands over his head like Dad does, which means he won't have all that hair for long. "Maybe there's something wrong with it."

Mia, Elaine, and I exchange glances.

Suddenly Elaine gasps. The blood drains from her face, and I think she's going to pass out. "You guys!" she cries. "We never called Shirley!"

This hits me nearly as hard as it does Elaine. How could I have forgotten to call Kit's mother? The General would have expected me to call Shirley first, not Mia. Kit's in the Intensive Care Unit, and Shirley doesn't even know it. She doesn't know she's a grandmother. I wonder as I race down the hall to the telephone if you keep being a grandmother even if your grandchild gets adopted. Is there a special contract for that?

I look up the number for Shirley's Place and dial. "Shirley?" The jukebox wails some corny country thing in the background.

"Speaking."

"This is Megan. I'm at the hospital. Kit's had her baby."

"What? Now? It's too soon! How is she? How's Kit?"

"Well"—I hesitate, wondering how much to tell her on the phone—"right now, she's in the Intensive Care—"

The receiver crashes to the bar. Shirley's yelling something hysterically, Kit's name, then something about locking up. The jukebox goes on about heartaches by the number, troubles by the score. Sometimes country makes a whole lot of sense.

We're not allowed inside Kit's room, not even Shirley. But there's a window, and an ICU nurse has pulled up the blinds. We line up, all six of us, and stare in. Lindsay holds on to Jonathan's arm with both hands as if she might topple over. Jonathan stands so close to the window that his breath condenses on the glass. Shirley says, "Oh, Lordie," and starts to sob, and Mia, of all people, puts an arm around her. Shirley leans her head against Mia's shoulder, thick black mascara running down her puffy cheeks.

Kit looks so tiny in that white bed. You can hardly see her face. There are tubes everywhere, blinking lights on high-tech machines, some red, some yellow like tiny winking eyes.

"Energy goes through glass," Elaine reminds us.

I concentrate all my positive thoughts, but it's hard. Kit looks so far away, like she's been stuck into a space capsule ready to leave the earth.

"I don't think we should give up hope," Lindsay says

in a small voice. "She's young, and you're very strong when you're young."

"Of course we're not giving up hope," Elaine says angrily, forgetting for a minute that Lindsay's an adult. "What a thing to say!"

"Oh, my poor kitten," Shirley sobs.

After a while the nurse sticks her head out and says time's up. "What Katherine needs now, more than anything," she says, "is complete rest."

"She's my only one," Shirley tries to explain, blotting at her runny mascara with a wadded-up tissue. "She's my baby, you know?"

The nurse, laying a hand on Shirley's arm, smiles and frowns at the same time. "Dr. Connors is taking Katherine's case," she says. "She's the best. You're lucky."

"Just one thing," Shirley pleads. "Call her Kit, okay? She just hates Katherine."

"Kit," the nurse says, giving Shirley's hand a quick squeeze. "Of course."

"Wait just a minute," Jonathan Keefe says, as the nurse turns to go back into Kit's room. "What's wrong with her, anyway? I mean, does she have some kind of"—his voice drops to a conspiratorial whisper as he tries to draw her away from the rest of us—"*you* know." He glances back at Shirley for a second. "Is it congenital or isn't it?"

"Excuse me," the nurse says sharply, becoming suddenly taller than her almost five feet, "but are you a relative?"

"Not exactly," Jonathan says, knocked a little back on his heels.

"Dr. Connors will have a full report in the morning," she says. "For the *family*."

"Can we see the baby?" Lindsay says. "Jonathan, ask her if we can see the *baby*!"

"You'll have to ask in PEDS," the nurse says tightly.

Lindsay and Jonathan head off in the direction of the elevator. Elaine, Mia, and I race for the stairs.

The General's at the desk filling in charts. She looks up, frowns. "Megan, you know you're not allowed up here!"

"They're coming," I cry, breathless from taking the stairs two at a time.

"Who? Who's coming?"

"The Keefes!" All that she doesn't know hits me like a slap to the side of the head.

"They're the ones Kit's giving the baby to," Mia explains.

"But they can't take her now," Elaine cries. "Can they, Mrs. Lane? I mean, Kit's not even . . . Kit could change her mind, couldn't she?"

"Girls!" says the General. "Calm down. No one's taking the baby. The baby's not going anywhere!"

The elevator doors slide open with a heavy sigh. Jonathan strides out, followed by Lindsay, hoop earrings flying.

"Jonathan Keefe," he says, stabbing his hand at the General. "We're the Clausen baby's adoptive parents."

"*Prospective* adoptive parents," Lindsay says, standing just a little behind her husband. "We'd like to see our baby"—she hesitates when the General doesn't return her smile—"if we possibly could."

I want to whap her with a magazine. "It isn't even legal, Mom!"

The General frowns at me, frowns at the Keefes.

"*Mom?*" Jonathan says. "What *is* this, some kind of conspiracy?"

"Nobody's signed anything!" I tell her. "There's no contract!"

"Quiet, Megan," the General says. "You're not helping."

The elevator doors wheeze open again, and out pops Shirley. I figured she'd gone for a cigarette or maybe a quick shot, but she was right behind us.

"This is the baby's grandma," I tell the General. "You remember Kit's mom, right?"

"Of course," the General says. "But I still don't know what all this is about. Apparently our children," she says to Shirley, stressing the word *children* and looking straight at me, "have been running the world in our absence."

"Is the baby all right?" Shirley says. When Shirley's sober, all she looks is tired, tired and kind of old. Her mascara's gone, and so is most of her lipstick. "I feel like one part of me is downstairs and the other part up here! Good Lord!" She drops her face into her hands. In her scoop-neck top, Shirley's shoulders look barely wired together.

The General comes around the desk. She guides Shirley away from the rest of us to a bank of plastic chairs and sits her down. "You have a darling little granddaughter," she says quietly, "but, as you probably know . . ."

I hear Shirley gasp.

"What?" Jonathan barks. "What's going on here? We have the right to know!"

The General turns. For a minute she doesn't say anything. She looks from Jonathan to Lindsay, strategizing. I've seen that look before. "I'll probably catch hell for this," she says finally. "Follow me, all of you."

We walk behind the General in a single line, down the corridor past rooms with closed doors and temporary name tags. The General stops at a supply closet. She begins passing out paper gowns, masks, gloves, bars of evil-smelling soap, and little plastic scrub brushes. "The bathroom's this way," she says. "Here," she says, handing me a stack of paper booties. "These go over your shoes." I pass them around. Everybody's very quiet. We take turns scrubbing our hands, help each other into our paper gowns. Mia whips her long hair on top of her head, twists it around a couple of times, and jams a pencil through to keep it in place.

"Two minutes," the General says, giving us the once-over. "I don't care whose baby it is!" She marches off down another hall. We follow, our paper slippers scuffing the slick linoleum. Lindsay looks frightened. Elaine is clearly thrilled. Mia squeezes my shoulder. I see her dark eyes smiling over the top of her mask. She seems to know something I don't.

"Wait right here," the General says. She goes into a room with an unmarked door and shuts it behind her. We wait. "Oh, God!" Lindsay says. "I think I'm going to faint."

"Not now," Jonathan orders.

The blinds go up, and the General appears. Next to her in a plastic isolette is Kit's baby, too tiny to be believed, her red face squinched and unhappy-looking. I know now what new parents mean when they say their baby's beautiful. I'd probably say the same thing about Kit's, but she isn't. She looks more or less like a hairless monkey. Shirley puts her hands on the window, both hands, and gazes down at her grandchild. "I just want to see her, memorize her," she says to Lindsay apologetically. "I know she's going with you."

My heart sinks. "No!" Elaine says.

The General sticks her head out. "One at a time," she says. "Shirley?"

Shirley takes a step, then looks at Lindsay, whose eyes are wide as half-dollars. "No," she says. "You should go first."

"Wait just a minute here!" Jonathan says, shoving Lindsay behind him. "Why all the caution? Is this child sick? Just tell me that."

The General gives him one of her famous bullet looks. "We don't know that yet, Mr. Keefe. She's been tested for HIV, but—"

"AIDS? Good God—AIDS? Are you saying this baby is infected?" Jonathan Keefe looks like he's about to run in three directions at once.

"That is *not* what I'm saying—"

But Jonathan isn't listening. "Lindsay, come away from that door!" he orders.

Lindsay stands uncertainly between the General and her husband. Over the mask her eyes look frightened and bewildered.

"Lindsay!" Jonathan rips off his mask. "If this baby has AIDS, it'll die. Is that what you want?"

Shirley has one of those cigarette voices, husky and deep. There are times when she uses it to great advantage. "You don't have a choice, Mr. Keefe," she says, stepping between Mom and the Keefes. "Not anymore you don't. This is *our* baby, Kit's and mine." She turns to the General. Their eyes meet in something I couldn't describe if I live to be a hundred.

"Come in and meet your grandchild, Shirley," the General says, like she knew just what would happen all along. Shirley sweeps through the door, her head high.

Lindsay pulls down her mask. Her eyes are bright with

tears. "You girls understand, don't you? It isn't that we wouldn't love the baby. . . ."

We turn away from Lindsay toward the window, where the General is helping Shirley fit her hands into the fat rubber gloves that reach into the isolette. We watch the way Kit's baby curls her teeny hand around her grandma's finger.

School isn't the real world after all, not today. Today the real world is happening in the ICU and in that little plastic isolette. In the real world, the hours tick off minute by minute until you get to twenty-four hours and the tests come back. In the real world, hours can seem like weeks.

At nutrition break, Elaine, Mia, and I head for Ms. Adams's office and beg to use her telephone. Finally we have to tell her why. She remembers Kit and shakes her head sadly. "Go ahead," she says. "One of you. The rest wait outside."

I dial with crossed fingers. "Stable," a woman's voice tells me.

"Stable as in good or—?"

"Stable," she says, "as in stable."

I replace the receiver and thank Ms. Adams. Only in prisons and public schools are telephones off-limits. An idea for my next story begins to percolate. "How To Tell If You're in Prison or High School: Ten Foolproof Tests."

"Give Kit my love." Ms. Adams sighs. "She's a sweet girl." Then in afterthought: "You all are. . . ."

"It was steroids," Elaine whispers in Bio. On the board Ms. Sato's scribbling a homework assignment that goes halfway across the room.

"*What* was steroids?" I watch Elaine poke away at Marilyn's drying heart. "Marilyn's on steroids?"

Elaine puts a finger to her lips. "Shhh!"

Ms. Sato turns, scans the room like RoboCop, turns back to the board.

I pull my stool closer to Elaine's.

"That's how Monk got it," she whispers. "He shared a needle with some other muscle-head."

"He didn't know he could get it by sharing a needle? Everybody knows that!"

Elaine rolls her eyes. "Everybody knows nothin'."

"Look, we've got to run it! If I hear one more thing . . . !"

Abe's on the computer playing around with next week's sports editorial. Technically it's not his job, but he loves resuscitating dead verbs. Instead of beating the opponent, the Taylor Tigers always trounce, batter, pummel, and flail. If we lose, which is more than half the time, Abe lets the dead verbs ride. "Everything you hear isn't necessarily news, Megan."

"Thanks for your support." I drop my backpack on the floor and slump into a desk. "Monk shared a needle. That's how he got it."

"Yeah, well, that's too bad. Dumb." Abe saves his

handiwork and leans back to admire it. "But, wearing my editor's hat so to speak, what's it got to do with running your article?"

"It's got to do with ignorance—that's what! It's the reason I wrote the article in the first place. If we don't know the risks, how can we make good choices?" I leap to my feet and start to pace, like Dad in the heat of battle. "Monk wants to be Mr. Universe, so he takes steroids. Well, it's his business, I guess, if he wants a short, beefed-up life. But it's mine when he infects my friend!"

I've got Abe's interest. He chews on the inside of his cheek. "We can't run it," he says finally.

"Why?" I stop in my tracks. "Cold feet?"

"Not hardly," Abe says with a short laugh. "The Wart's got it."

"So? It's still on the hard drive."

"It's also in print," Abe says. "In this week's *Trib*. Camera ready. On the Wart's desk. He's refusing to sign off on it and without his signature no printer in town will touch it."

"You actually did it? You put in my story?"

"Sure. It's good stuff. It needs to get out there." The printer spits out the first page of the sports article. Abe scans it quickly.

"What did Ms. Espinosa say?"

The look on his face tells me. She doesn't know. She's our adviser and we're supposed to get her approval for everything, but she's new and I guess you could say we've taken advantage of that.

I sigh the way the General sighs at the end of a long hard shift. "So. No signature, no paper."

"There's nothing I can do," Abe says glumly.

"Are you sure you've thought of absolutely every-thing?"

Abe gives me a dark look. "What are you hatching, Megan?"

"It's just a thought. . . ."

"Yes?"

"Well, I was just wondering if all the printers in town know the Wart's signature? I mean, they couldn't. Could they?"

Abe's eyes widen. "You wouldn't," he says. "That's forgery, Megan. Not to mention breaking and entering."

"Breaking and entering?"

"The Wart's office. Can't sign it unless we get our hands on it."

Holding our breath, we each think it through. The challenge. The excitement. The terror.

The punishment.

"Naaaah," I say. Abe can't hide his relief. "I've got another idea."

"What?"

"Have you ever heard the saying that it's better to ask forgiveness than to beg for permission?"

Abe chews on this. "What are you up to, Megan?"

"You'll see."

Our booth at the Coffee Cat is empty without Kit. Mia lights up. Elaine chews a cuticle. We sip our coffee. Nobody says much. Every once in a while one of us gets up and calls the hospital. Stable, every time. Like a broken record. After a while a nurse wises up and recognizes it's the same three voices calling. We're reminded that time on the telephone is time away from patients.

We take turns trying to change the subject. "So," Elaine says, "you and Joe going to the prom?"

Joe seems like somebody I knew in a previous life. I shrug. "I don't know. I guess."

Elaine stirs her mocha till all the whipped cream's gone. The girl at the register sings a Sheryl Crow song through her nose ring, off-key and loud.

This month's wall art is all about people losing their eyeballs and other essential body parts, done in globs of purple and olive green with occasional splashes of yellow-orange. There are fliers for a Retro Poetry Reading and Aura Analysis. Toad the Wet Sprocket is doing a last concert before their big tour. There's a volleyball championship this weekend at the beach, sponsored by Budweiser.

In the real world, kids just have fun. Don't they?

"I've been thinking a lot about Hawaii lately," Mia says, smoke drifting from her nose. "Things are—I don't know—simple there, you know?"

We don't know, and she can't exactly explain. What she explains, or tries to explain, is the color of the water. "Like a bluie," she says.

"A bluie?" Elaine says.

"The marble, dummy! Didn't you guys ever play marbles? It's blue like that, like you can see straight through it." She rolls an imaginary marble between her fingers, and we all look through it. "And the air smells like flowers. All the time, not just like on holidays or something." Her eyes go dreamy like she's seeing the Big Island in her head. "I wish you guys could go with me this summer."

We dream along, picturing water the color of a bluie.

"Maybe you can!" Mia says. "I've got a dozen aunties over there. At least!"

"But what about Kit?" Elaine says. A cloud sails over our imaginary island.

"Time to call," I say. "It's been twenty minutes."

I phone Joe after the General and Dad turn in. I look up his number in the phone book and dial it, just like that. Just like he's any old ordinary human being, which he is. He sounds surprised to hear my voice and, I think, pleased. "What's up? You never call me."

"Yeah, well, I've been busy."

"So I've heard."

I plunk down on my bed. Spoof groans. "What have you heard?"

"Three guesses. Did you really think you could keep the deal with Kit quiet? Where do you think we're living? L.A.? How's she doing?"

"Not so good. She's what they call 'stable.' She had a little girl, Joe."

"Neat!" he says, and then, as an afterthought, "Well, sort of. I guess."

We listen for the pin to drop. It never does.

Finally I bring up why I called. "About the prom?"

"Yeah?"

"I know I said I'd go but—I don't know—with all this going on—"

"Yeah . . ."

"You don't mind?"

"Sure I mind. I think we should go. Kit can't be your whole entire life, Megan."

Where have I heard that before?

"Besides, I already bought the tickets," he says.

"You did? Both of them?"

"Well, yeah, sure. Reserved a tux, too. What did'ja think? I'm a slouch?"

"Joe?"

"Megan?"

"Wanna do me a favor?"

"Several. Top to bottom."

"I'm serious. Can you keep a secret?"

Copy Your Heart Out sits in an island of dazzling light in the middle of a huge nearly empty parking lot. Joe pulls into a space, and we hop out. Joe looks awfully good. It makes my lips itch just to look at him. He even holds the door. "Let me read it first," he says.

"No way!" Inside, the place is buzzing like it's being run by invisible insect robots. I grab a meter and head for a copy machine. "You staple."

Joe punches the stapler to see if it's up to his usual standards. He staples X's in a neat row across the bottom of his T-shirt. "Are you sure you know what you're doing?" he says.

"Nope, I don't. Want out?"

"Did I say that?"

"Don't worry," I assure him with dead seriousness. "No one will know you're responsible for the staples."

I find the copy of "Teen Sex: Get It While It's Hot. Or Not." and a marking pen in my backpack. In bold black letters, I write across the top: THIS IS WHAT YOUR SCHOOL ADMINISTRATION DOESN'T WANT YOU TO KNOW. The pen hesitates over my name but doesn't cross it out.

"Jeez!" Joe says, reading over my shoulder. "Sex. It's about sex! You'll never get away with it."

I plug the counter in. "Got some money?"

"Some."

"Good, 'cause this is going to cost!"

"I hope you know what you're doing, Megan," he says.

"Sure," I say. "It's easy. Watch! All you do is lay the copies facedown—"

"You know what I mean," Joe says.

At night Taylor looks peaceful. Like it's resting from all the noise and chaos of the day. The seagulls and the janitors have done their job. The quad is clean, an almost friendly square of concrete with a few scattered benches. A place to sit and ponder the Great Questions of Existence, of life and death. I head for the lockers.

"Woah!" says Joe. I turn and catch him reading. " 'A broken heart is one thing; a broken condom is another. Take the following test to see how much you know. True or False: A girl can't get pregnant if she's having her period.' " He looks up. "Everybody knows the answer to that, don't they?"

"Do you?"

"Of course I do."

I wait.

"Well, she can, right? She *can* get pregnant."

"Are you sure?"

"Megan Lane, are you trying to undermine my sexual self-confidence?"

"Fat chance of that."

It takes Joe and me no more than half an hour to stuff lockers and slide copies under all the classroom doors. For good measure, I shove three under the door of the Admin building. "What if you get kicked out of school?" Joe says when the last article's been stuffed into the last locker. "Did you think about that?"

"I'm already grounded—what's the difference?"

"There's a difference," he says as we head for the car.

A shiver goes straight up my back. "I know."

Joe stops a block from my house and cuts the engine. "I don't know about this idea of yours," he says. "But I'm glad you called."

Joe's pickup cools down with little pings and clicks. "Me, too." I don't tell him I could just as easily have called Mia, or Elaine for that matter. But I didn't want to get them in trouble.

"If I tell you something, will you promise not to, you know, take it wrong?"

"Nope."

Joe checks me out to see if I'm kidding. He shakes his head. "Okay, I'll tell you anyway. It's about you. It's something I've been thinking about, but it's kind of hard to explain." Joe watches his hands fidget with the steering wheel, rocking it back and forth.

"Yeah?" My voice comes out shakier than I intended it to. It seems like I'm being told off a lot these days.

"You're, well . . . you're not just a girl, you know?"

"Gee, thanks," I say flatly.

"Hang on—I'm trying to explain." He risks meeting my eyes. "You're different—that's all. You're not silly, not all, like . . . dumb, giggly! Worried about your makeup. Well, that's not it exactly. Anyway"—he checks out his hands again, I guess to make sure they haven't dropped off the ends of his wrists—"I like you. I *admire* you, I guess is what I'm trying to say."

"Well, thanks," I say. "I guess. I admire Walter Cronkite, but I wouldn't take him to the prom."

"I still want to, you know, make it with you. Don't get me wrong!"

"Well, *that's* a relief."

"Hey!" he says, hands up as if he's surrendering. "I'm only being honest!"

7:50 A.M. and the quad is full of kids. Some are sitting on benches, the few there are. Some are sprawled on the grass. Some are just standing around in little groups, more or less like any other day. The difference is that they're quiet. And they're reading. They're reading the article. "Teen Sex . . ." is everywhere. I feel my face heat up and head for the girls' room. It's full. I duck back out. "Hey, Megan, nice work!" someone says as I hurry toward the *Trib* room. Other kids swivel their heads as I dash by and say nothing at all.

The *Trib* room is empty. Only the flat gray eyes of a half dozen computers face me as I close the door and lean against it, heart hammering, ears ringing. Last night's bravado melts like a snow cone in a heat wave. I don't want to be famous, or should I say infamous? The door suddenly opens and I topple backward into Ms. Espinosa. "Megan?" She supports me while I regain my balance. "I guess I don't have to ask what you're doing in here." She slips out of her cardigan sweater and drapes it carefully over the back of the teacher's chair. She looks up. Her brown eyes are level with mine. "Why don't you tell me what you had in mind?" she says quietly. "I'm curious."

"Freedom of the press," I say, a nice ring of conviction in my voice.

"And if the *Tribune* gets cut? What then, Megan? Then what happens to your freedom of the press?"

"Cut?"

"That didn't occur to you."

"No."

"Nor did lawsuits, I assume."

"Well—"

"Or people's jobs. Mine, for example."

"They wouldn't—"

"I'm a new teacher, Megan. I'm still on probation. And I'm responsible for what goes on here. Not you, not Abe. Me." Ms. Espinosa's a single mom with three kids.

"Well, I'm sorry. I really am, but somebody's got to say what's going on. Somebody's got to let kids know what's happening!"

"In a school-sponsored newspaper."

"Where else?"

She sighs, takes down the long pole, and starts opening the windows. "It's a clever article, Megan. I might even say well written. But the facts are questionable, your research shoddy—"

"I was objective! I didn't tell anybody what to think. I just reported what people said!"

She replaces the pole. She sighs. "You wrote that article for yourself, Megan. To show how smart you are." The bright sunlight makes her squint like she's in pain. "Well, congratulations," she says. "You're smart. Now what?"

* * *

The yellow slip comes in the middle of Bio. It's like everybody, not just me, has been waiting for it. Everything comes to a stop. Pencils pause; bug stickers stick. Ms. Sato calls my name. Elaine squeezes my hand. I get up, leaving the floor of my stomach behind. I feel like Marilyn, splayed and about to be quartered. Ms. Sato hands me the pass with absolutely no expression on her face. She's the soul of scientific objectivity, but that's hard to appreciate right now.

I head out the door. The sun is still in the sky. The world's still out there where I left it. Things go right on no matter what happens to Megan Lane. The seagulls have flown in for their nutrition break. They squawk and bicker over cookie crumbs and pizza crusts. I stop to pick up a page of my article that has a big footprint stamped across it. Abe catches up, matching his stride to mine. His tie swings loose. Abe's known for his ties, the only boy in school who wears one. "Nice tie," I say.

"I chose it carefully for the current political climate," he says grimly.

"I see." The tie is black with hot orange Tabasco bottles on it.

We sit on the bad kids' bench outside the Wart's door watching Mrs. True's hands turn chartreuse at the copy machine. "You've never done anything wrong," Abe assures me. "He'll just give you a warning."

"Then why are my hands shaking?"

"It's part of the deal," he says. "You're supposed to sweat. He's probably in there munching on donuts, but he's gotta make you wait. Make you sweat."

The door snaps open. The Wart sticks his head out. "Come in here, Megan." He turns and stomps back inside.

I get up like I'm going to the Chair. I go into the Wart's office.

Abe follows me in. The Wart scowls at Abe. "What are you doing here?"

"I'm her editor," Abe says in his Spencer Tracy voice.

"Was it your idea to distribute that article?"

Abe hesitates. "No, but—"

"But what? Butt out! This isn't your business. Back to class, young man." Abe goes to the door but seems to have forgotten how to open it.

"I'd offer you a seat, Megan," the Wart says, "but this isn't a hearing. It isn't a trial. You're suspended. Three days. I've already heard from CSR. CRS. Whatever they are. Those mothers! You'll be lucky if I don't slap on another three days by the time we're through hearing about this!"

I turn and stumble past Abe, who's holding the door for me. Through my tears, Mrs. Beamis and Mrs. True are a jumble of color, like figures in a fun house mirror. Behind me I hear Abe arguing and the Wart threatening Abe with suspension.

Outside the office, I don't know where to go, where to find myself. I go around the side of the building to the faculty parking lot. Suspended.

Excluded.

Shut out.

Dismissed. Discharged. Sent packing.

Megan Lane, suspended! How can that be?

I slide down the side of the rough brick wall and let the tears go. If we only get a certain number of tears to cry in a lifetime, I've used mine up in just a few weeks. The sleeves of Danny's sweatshirt are soft against my face.

Thinking about Danny makes me cry even harder. Abe crouches beside me, elbows on his knees. "Megan Lane, Ace Reporter," he says, "Dissolves in Faculty Parking Lot Deluge."

I wipe my eyes and nose on my sleeve. I'm not prepared for breaking down on a daily basis, and the shirt is all I have. I try being philosophical. "Well, now I'll have time for Kit."

"Only a couple of days," Abe says. "Enough to feel deep and abiding shame." Abe holds a hand over his heart and rolls his eyes dramatically. "Then you're supposed to turn a new page."

"So to speak."

Abe gives my hand a surprising little squeeze. I don't pull away; neither does he. "So to speak," he says.

We head for Bio so Abe can get back to class and I can retrieve my backpack. Heads are down as we enter the room, everybody so into their frog you'd think they were making soup. Thirty-five pairs of eyes watch as I pick up my backpack. I sling it over one shoulder, looking, I hope, braver than I feel. Elaine mouths, "Suspended?" She's so pale I think she might pass out. I nod and head for the door.

The applause startles me. I turn, and every kid in the room is standing up, clapping. No one yells. No one says, "Way to go, Megan!" or punches the air. They just stand there and applaud, some smiling, some with serious faces, Elaine in tears. Ms. Sato is startled into silence. I love every one of them right then, even Ms. Sato.

"Suspended? What do you mean, suspended?" The General stops dead in the middle of her bedroom, panty hose wrapped around her knees.

"I can explain!" I launch straight into the First Amendment: " 'Congress shall make no law respecting the establishment of religion, or prohibiting the free exercise thereof; or abridging the freedom of speech, or of the press . . . '!" My voice rings like Dad's when he argues for a client who's been wronged by the system.

The General wriggles her panty hose the rest of the way up, gets a run, and yanks them off. "You have gone too far this time, young lady!" Barefooted, she stomps over to her dresser and pulls out a drawer. There, like a nest of brown eggs, are all her neatly rolled pairs of panty hose. She grabs one and stretches it up to the light. "You are barely sixteen years old. You *have* no First Amendment rights!" In her pink sponge curlers and avocado beauty mask, she's more than a little scary. "Good Lord, Megan, what were you thinking? Or *were* you thinking? Obviously not!" She whips on the new panty hose, snaps them into place at her waist. "Did it occur to you how this would reflect on us, your family? And what about your school record? What about college? Did you think about that? How your *reputation* might precede you there?"

She doesn't expect answers.

She pads over to her closet, grabs a uniform, flings it onto the bed. At a safe distance, I follow her into her bathroom and watch her rinse her face. She comes up out of the sink blubbering. "Suspended! I can't believe it!"

"You're supposed to call the Wart," I tell her.

"Who?"

"Mr. Wartner."

She slathers her face with lotion. Our eyes meet in the mirror. "Megan?"

"Yes, ma'am."

"I will not tolerate disrespect. For anyone."

"No, ma'am."

"And," she says, shooting me the old bullet, "I don't like surprises!"

"No, ma'am."

"Don't be smart!"

"I'm not being smart."

"Think about the school board!" she says.

"Huh?"

"I'll probably be asked to resign!" She yanks the pink sponges out of her hair. Her curls stand up in little round tunnels. "First this thing with Kit and now this! I'm beginning to think I don't know my own daughter!" She slaps on her foundation. In three minutes she's in full makeup. *Glamour*'s got nothing on the General. She yanks a brush through her curls, and she's finished.

160

I follow her back into the bedroom. She steps into her uniform skirt and ties on her nurse's shoes. I've never seen her polish them but, somehow, they're always spotless. She buttons her smock and checks her full-length mirror with the usual frown. The General's her own drill sergeant, permanently dissatisfied. She pins her badges on.

"Think about it this way, Mom," I suggest philosophically. "None of this counts, not really."

She turns ever so slowly from the mirror to me, a dangerous half-smile on her face. "By which you mean the fact that you have been kicked out of high school like a common criminal."

"Suspended, that's all. For three days. Big deal. It's Kit that matters, Mom. Kit and the baby. What's a few days' suspension to the possibility of being HIV-positive?"

"Megan?" The General's green eyes snap and spark; her curls stand on end. She grows three feet taller in the blink of an eye. The air in the room begins to spin. I back away.

"Yes, ma'am?"

"Go to your room, young lady! This minute! Do *not* say another word. Do *not* come out of your room until I tell you to!" I hustle right out of there. She slams the door behind me. She opens it again and yells down the hall, "Until June!" Her door slams again.

Civilized people don't slam doors. She'll tell you that herself.

"You have put your principal in a hell of a position, Megan." Dad sighs, dialing the telephone. He frowns a little, waiting for someone to answer. I'm so relieved that he's the one calling the Wart. The General would sell me straight down the river. "Yes, I'll hold. Howard Lane— that's right." He's using his lawyer voice. I remember how he shut the coach down. The Wart doesn't have a chance.

Dad taps his fingers lightly on the arms of his chair. He looks out the window onto the side yard, where the General has recently placed a white plaster angel. Dad says it appears that we now have our own private cemetery. The General was not amused. She got it for a song, she said. Dad reminded her that singing has never been one of her talents. "Mr. Wartner, yes. Howard Lane. Megan's father." His forehead bunches up in concentration. "Yes. Mmmm . . . Uh-huh . . . Well, of course." He listens some more. I wonder when he's going on the defense. "Impulsive? Well . . . perhaps. Yes, she certainly can be strong-willed at times." His eyes meet mine, daring argument. Is *he* selling me down the river? "She gets that from her mother's side," he says, straight-faced. Aha, I think, a little humor and then he goes in for the kill. "Three days? Seems fair. Certainly . . . Yes, yes. Of course."

"Daddy!" I leap to my feet and grab his arm. I can't believe my ears!

He fends me off. "Not at all, Mr. Wartner. Mrs. Lane and I appreciate your position." He replaces the receiver and turns to me. "What did you expect, Megan?"

I'm shocked speechless.

"You defied school authority."

"I told the truth!"

"In an underhanded way, yes. Did you even try publishing your article elsewhere? No." Like the General, he can answer all his own questions. No wonder they're married. "Did you ask if you could distribute the story on your own, as a student and not a representative of the school newspaper? No? Well"—he shrugs—"as the saying goes, Do the crime; do the time. What can I say?"

"Thanks a lot!" I cry. "Thanks a whole hell of a lot! What good does it do to have a lawyer for a father if he won't even stand up for your rights!"

"Careful, Megan," he warns.

"Well, it's not fair! You always say to tell the truth, but when I do, I get busted for it!"

"If you *had* rights in this case, Megan, believe me I'd defend them. I have before. Now," he says pointedly, "*if* you want to challenge the school district legally, take on the issue of students' rights to speech and press. . . . Do a little research . . . make the system work for you. See what needs to be done. . . ."

I haul my old ten-speed, covered with dust, out of the garage. The tires are flat, and a spider has built her home between the spokes of my front wheel. Making the system work for her, Dad would say. Furiously I pump the front tire. The bike shakes, and the web wobbles. Finally the spider, disgusted, makes her way to the ground and stomps off.

As I ride, I think about that—about the spider, about the system, about what Dad said. It's a long way to Cottage Hospital, with lots of stops and hills and turns, and there's plenty of time to think. I pass Joe's house. The light's on in his room.

What if the Wart found out Joe helped? Would Joe be suspended, too?

Could Ms. Espinosa really lose her job?

Is Abe on the Wart's hit list?

Will one kid think before having unprotected sex? Or having sex at all?

Am I just a busybody?

Is it all worth it?

I stop at a gas station ladies' room near the hospital and lean my bike against the wall. Inside, I lock the door behind me and shuck off my backpack. In the cold yellowish light of the bathroom, my face in the mirror looks crazed.

The wig is left over from some Halloween years ago. It's pitch-black, almost as long as Mia's, and 100 percent synthetic. Pulled back in a ponytail, it looks almost normal. I fish in my backpack for the rest of the stuff. The dress came from the dark inner recesses of my closet, way back with the hideous things "too good to give away," according to the General. It's blue-checkered, like Dorothy's in *The Wizard of Oz*. I step into it and button it up. It's tight. Too many Oreos. Buttons will pop unless I hold my breath. The patent leather pumps and the hose are the General's. So is the dark red lipstick, which I apply just a little over the lip lines for effect.

I check myself in the mirror. Eighteen, easy. I stuff my jeans, shirt, and shoes in my backpack. I poke my head outside, check for whoever might have seen me go in a kid and out a woman. One old guy with his head under the hood of some old wreck. Safe.

I climb on the bike and almost fall off.

I try again and this time manage riding with the pumps the two blocks to Cottage. I stow my bike and backpack behind a hedge near the entrance.

The lobby is nearly empty. A man sleeps sitting up,

his mouth hung open. A large woman in flowered silk leafs through *People*. At the reception desk at the far end of the room is the volunteer pink lady. She's about a hundred years old, and, if I'm lucky, she's nearsighted. Once past her, I'm in.

My heart thuds. My ears ring. I know that the General's in and out of this lobby all the time, escorting newly released mothers and babies to waiting cars. I could fool a hundred people but not the General. Like a mother bear, she'd detect me by smell.

The pink lady looks up from her newspaper. "How may I help?" she says sweetly.

"That's okay!" I say, breezing by. "I know right where I'm going."

She raises a hand as if she's about to ask a question. I head for the elevator. It takes its sweet time.

In the elevator a little boy looks up at me with wary eyes and moves closer to his mother. You can fool a hundred people a hundred ways, but you can't fool kids.

ICU. Gray walls and carpet, a silvery silence. Not a soul around. I head for Kit's room, down the hallway to the right. All this time I've been picturing Kit, the Kit of a few days ago, the Kit of before all this, just cracking up when she sees me.

Elaine says laughter can cure anything, even cancer. At a dimly lit station between the two hallways, a nurse hunkers down over a pile of charts. She doesn't look up as I sneak past, holding my breath.

At the far end of the hall is Kit's room, the only one brightly lit. I figure it's a good sign.

The blinds are up. The light is so bright it hurts. The bed is made the way they do, with sheets overlapping sheets, white on white.

Kit's not in it.

You can hear your heart when it breaks, if you listen real close.

And then you just start shaking.

"May I help you?" It's the nurse who stood right up to Jonathan Keefe. "Visitors are not allowed back here."

She watches me suspiciously as I try to work my mouth. Finally my voice comes out in a rusty squeak. "Kit . . . she's my friend. Please . . . did she . . . ? Is Kit dead?" A button pops off my Dorothy dress and rolls off down the floor.

"Oh, my dear, no!" She turns me gently by the elbow, all the time looking at me strangely, as if she might have seen me someplace before. Like in the psych ward. "Katherine's in Maternity. She's doing just fine."

I head for the elevator in a wobble-run. "South wing!" she calls, but I know this hospital like I know my own house.

"Megan?" The curtain's pulled to one side, and Kit's bed's cranked up. I recognize one of my old flannel shirts, Danny's flannel shirts, red-and-gray plaid with holes in the elbows. It's half-unbuttoned. At Kit's tiny breast, which isn't so tiny now, is Monkey-face. "You look weird! What have you got on?"

"Never mind," I say. "I thought they wouldn't let me in." I don't know where to sit or stand. I don't know what to do with my hands or what to say. I'm so relieved I could cry, but I'm probably out of tears by now. "Are you all right? Well, I mean I guess you are if . . ."

"Isn't she beautiful?" Kit says, her blue eyes shining like she's in love, which I guess she is.

I nod. Does anybody tell the truth?

"Oh, Megan, can you believe I almost gave her away?" She cups the baby's bald head like a softball with her free hand. Kit's shrunk, which I guess I should have expected. She's her old self. Except, of course, that she isn't her old self. She'll never be her old self again.

I have to ask, only I don't know quite how. "Are you, you know . . . *okay?*"

Kit gives me a quizzical look. "Oh," she says, laughing. "*That!* No! We're fine." She looks down at the baby and says in a sugary baby voice, "We don't have that nasty HIV stuff, do we, sweetie pie? Unnh-uh, not us!" She smiles up at me like she's easily dodged a bad case of the flu.

I try smiling back, but my mouth's stuck.

"Can you believe it? My own baby! It's the most wonderful thing that ever happened to me!"

The baby yawns, her little mouth in the perfect letter *O*, and snorts through her nose.

"And guess what? Shirley's going to sell the bar and open up a children's clothing store. Like, you know, used clothes?"

"Neat," I say.

"You don't seem very excited." Kit pouts.

Shirley? Selling baby clothes? "I'm just . . . surprised, that's all."

Megan gives me a disgusted look. "People change, Megan. They aren't perfect, but they can change."

"Well, sure. . . ."

"Want to hold her?" Kit pops the baby off the nipple. The teeny mouth sucks air for a second. Then she drops off to sleep, just like that. "You have to wash your hands real good first."

Soaping my hands, I catch a glimpse of myself in the mirror and nearly yelp in fright. I peel off the wig and wash my face. I put on my jeans and shirt.

Kit's got the baby tightly wrapped, her little round face the only part showing. I sit carefully on the edge of the bed, and Kit transfers the tiny bundle to me. I'm amazed that she can do this and that I can just take the baby from her. Like a football, not a real live infant human being.

The baby's light as breath. She smells warm and milky like a kitten. With stiff arms, I hold her close to my chest and search her sleeping face for signs of Kit. Or Monk. But she's her own little person, at least so far. "Does she have a name yet?"

"Uh-huh," says Kit, like that's never been a problem.

"So, what is it?"

"You might not like it."

"What?"

"Megan." Kit laughs. "Her name is Megan. Megan Lynn Clausen."

"You're kidding! You'd name a kid Megan?"

"After you," Kit says. "After my best friend. What's wrong with that?"

I gaze down at Megan with new respect. Megan Clausen. At least it doesn't sound like the name of a street.

"I guess that makes you her godmother," Kit says. "I mean if that's all right with you."

I almost say, "Sure!" the way I always do with Kit, but something stops me. "I don't have a godmother, Kit. Do you?"

"Nope. I just thought, well . . ."

But she didn't think, not really. Kit isn't into thinking, at least not for long.

"What does it mean, anyway? To be a godmother."

Kit shrugs. She's already lost interest. Her eyes wander up to the TV, where Vanna, in white sequins, flips a *W* into place.

With a sigh worthy of the General, I pass Megan back to Kit. "Cinderella's godmother turned Cinderella into an instant princess."

"Yeah, well, that's just a fairy tale," Kit says. "I'll be happy if Megan graduates from high school!"

"You're coming back to school, right?"

I notice for the first time how much older Kit looks, as if she's aged ten years, a not-very-happy ten years.

"I dunno," she says. "Things are different now. It just wouldn't be the same."

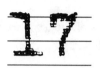

"Megan?"

"Yeah?"

"Monk."

I nearly drop the receiver.

"Hey, could you meet me? Just for a minute. Somewhere. Anywhere." All the wind's gone out of Monk—you can hear it in his voice.

"Sure. Where?"

"How about the park? The bandstand, you know . . ."

"Where we used to skate."

"Yeah. But, hey"—his laugh is forced—"don't bring those stupid clamp-on skates."

Monk's sitting on the bandstand steps when I get there, hunched over his knees. "Hey, kid," he says, looking up, "thanks for coming."

"Sure." I shrug.

He pats the step beside him. "Have a seat," he says with a sad half-smile. "It's safe."

I hesitate. Not because he's HIV-positive—I know better—but because he's all the other things. A senior, Tiffany's boyfriend, captain of the basketball team, the Great Monk. But none of that matters much now. I sit beside him.

Monk's wearing a jeans jacket with the collar turned up. The blond spikes of his crew cut glimmer. In the distance, moms push kids on swings. A chubby dark-haired boy plays soccer with himself, kicking his ball from one tree to the next.

"I want you to give Kit something for me," Monk says. "You know, for the baby."

"Megan," I tell him.

He looks at me strangely, as if I'm talking to myself.

"The baby's name is Megan."

"Oh. And that's, you know, okay with you?"

"Sure. I guess. Why wouldn't it be?"

"I dunno." Monk shrugs. "I was named after my old man—"

"Your *dad's* name is Monk?"

"Martin," he says. "And I was Little Marty. Jeez!" He rolls his eyes.

"So how did you get to be Monk?"

"Well," he says slowly, as if deciding whether or not to go on. "Up until, well . . . for a long time, I wanted to be a priest. Or my ma wanted me to be one. Same thing."

"Really?"

Monk a priest? Does the pope play basketball?

"Yeah. But then"—he shrugs—"it started looking like priests didn't have all that much fun."

"Oh."

"But"—he scowls—"I never heard of a priest getting AIDS, either."

Monk pulls an envelope out of his back pocket. It's folded in half and looks like it's been sat on for a while. "I was going to take this over myself," he says, "but I couldn't. It's not just the old lady"—he taps the envelope lightly against his palm before passing it to me—"it's Kit. When I first . . . when we first . . . well, it seemed like just a good time, you know? She was willing, she was pretty cute . . . aw, shit!" He throws his head back for a minute and squeezes his eyes shut. "Anyway," he says, looking back at me, "I can't do it. I want you to give that to her. Will you?"

"Well, sure. But don't you want to see the baby? I mean, just once?"

"Would *you*?" Monk's blue eyes bore into mine with an intensity that makes me squirm. "Think about it, Megan. Every single day I say good-bye to more stuff! Well, not *stuff*. That's easy. The money in that envelope is from the Mustang. Can't believe how easy that was! I could have *given* it away if it wasn't for Kit needing the money. It's people I can't say good-bye to . . . Mom, Tiff . . ."

"Is Tiffany . . . ?"

He looks away. I watch his jaw clench. Tiffany, Queen of Everything, HIV-positive.

"But maybe the next test . . . in six months . . . ?"

He shakes his head. "It's been six months," he says. "Six months, three weeks, and"—he counts—"five days. Tiff and I went together for our tests. Just like we were getting a marriage license or something." He seems to shake himself mentally.

The soccer ball rolls to the bottom step and stops. Monk

172

leans down, picks it up. He twirls it like a basketball on his finger. The boy looks up in awe. "Hey," he says. "Wanna play?"

Monk doesn't say anything. He just looks at the little boy with this faraway look in his eyes, like he's seeing himself as a kid starting all over again. "Some other time," he says softly, and tosses the ball back. He looks over at me. "I don't hear from anybody—you know that? Only Tiff, and that's . . . hard, you know?"

How can I know? But I nod as if I do.

"It's like I'm this . . . *thing!* This leper." He looks down at his clasped hands. He looks so strong, so alive.

"Maybe nobody, you know, really believes it."

He shakes his head. "I hardly believe it myself. I didn't even know what a T cell was six months ago; now I could write the book on them."

The sun slips behind a cloud, and it's suddenly cool. The moms begin packing up. I burrow down into my pockets, wishing I knew the right things to say.

"I didn't think I wanted to know, but I guess I do. Do they have it?"

"Kit and Megan? No, they're fine."

Monk puts his face in his hands. He doesn't look up for a long time, and when he does, his eyes are wet. He starts to say something but shakes his head and looks away.

"She doesn't blame you for anything," I say, making things up as I go along. "She's just happy the baby's okay."

"God, it's funny how things change. Maybe it's me. Maybe it's me changing. Everything *hurts* so much. . . . I didn't know it hurt so much to care. Is that dumb or what?"

"It isn't dumb." My throat is thick with tears.

"Well, hey! I didn't mean to lay all this on you." He

stands up, stuffs his hands into his back pockets. "Just . . . tell her . . . tell Kit . . . I don't know. Damn! Just tell her she's a good kid; tell her I'm sorry. The money"—he shrugs—"Kit and the baby will need it." He turns away, turns back again. "And you," he says, pretending to frown. "You take care of yourself."

I watch him till he leaves the park, until he's a blue speck in the distance, a blue speck with a yellow halo.

"All she does is cry!" whines Kit. Little Megan straddles Kit's shoulder, her red face squinched up in misery. "I feed her, I burp her, I change her, I walk her. . . ." Kit lays Megan in her bassinet. Megan starts to wail.

"Here, let me hold her." I reach into the bassinet but suddenly lose my nerve. "You pick her up. Then I'll hold her."

Kit pops Megan right out of the bassinet and dumps her in my arms. She's warm and damp and squirming like crazy, kicking and yelling against my chest.

Kit drops into a rocking chair Lindsay sent before the baby was born, her legs splayed out. Except for the flat belly, she looks the same as she did when she was pregnant, tired and pale and kind of dissatisfied with everything. Any silly ideas that the old Kit might return to us go up in smoke. She's been wearing the same baggy shirt for a week. She's forgotten how to laugh. Would she sing Patsy Cline tunes to Megan? I didn't think so.

I walk the room in circles, bouncing the yelling baby. After a while she starts to wind down; then she's asleep. Kit pries her carefully from my sopping shoulder and lays her in the bassinet.

"I saw Monk today."

Kit's eyes widen.

"He said to give you this." I hand her the envelope, warm from my pocket.

She looks at it like it might blow up. Then she takes it, tears it open. She unfolds a yellow check. "Wow," she says quietly.

"He sold his car."

She looks up, surprised. "The mean green Mustang?" She reads the numbers on the check several times. Then she folds it and drops it on the dresser. "Well, it's nice, but it's not gonna send anybody's mama to college," she says.

"Is that all you think about?"

"College? Me? Hardly."

"No, I mean *you*. Is that all you think about? You. Yourself."

"Hey, lighten up! I was kidding."

"That was all Monk owned in the world, Kit. You know how he loved that car! Now he's just . . . he's just saying good-bye to things!"

"Yeah, well . . . ," she says dryly.

"Yeah, well, what? Serves him right? That's what you're thinking, right?" I can feel myself heating up.

"Well, doesn't it?"

"AIDS? Who deserves AIDS? Kit, it could have been you!"

"Oh, give me a break, Megan!"

18

It's the General's forty-fifth. I had to count them up myself—she wouldn't tell me. Dad's squeezing oranges; I'm waiting for bubbles to pop on the blueberry pancakes so I can flip them over. "I'll bet she's awake," he says. "But I hope we surprise her."

"Dad, is a godparent, you know, like a legal thing?"

"Hmmm," he says, pouring orange juice. "No. It's not a legally binding agreement. Unless somebody signs something. Why?"

"Kit wants me to be Megan's godmother."

He frowns a little. "I see."

"But I don't know. . . ."

"It's something to think about," he says. "I wouldn't rush into it, if I were you."

"What would I have to do?"

"Well, you wouldn't *have* to do anything. But in some

families godparents are, well, kind of next in line. If something should happen to the parents. Or they do really special things on birthdays. Or pay for college, I suppose, in the event the parents can't do that. But, as I've said, if there isn't a contract . . ."

"A legal contract, you mean."

He raises his eyebrows the way he does when he's teasing. "What other kind is there?"

"You know what kind," I say. "The kind you don't sign. Moral contracts, I guess you call them."

"Ah!" he says. "You're learning, kiddo. Here, take this tray. Wait! Let's throw in some more of this."

"But the General doesn't eat bacon!" I say with a straight face.

"*Right!*" says Dad.

The phone rings. "Megan?"

Kit.

"Megan, I forgot to tell you something. Before, when you were here."

I wait.

"Promise you won't get mad."

"Just tell me." I sigh. I lay my head down on Spoofus. His fat belly wheezes up and down like an accordion.

"I'm going to ask Lindsay to be Megan's godmother."

"Great!"

"Oh, I *knew* you'd be mad!"

"No, I mean it, Kit. It's a great idea. Lindsay's perfect!"

I feel suddenly light as air, like I could float right up off the bed. I didn't think Lindsay would accept, but what do I know, really?

"Megan?"

"Yeah?"

"You're still my very best friend."

"I know, Kit."

"Zip me," Mia says. She holds up a pile of shining black hair while I zip. "Are you sure this is okay?"

"Okay?" the General says. "It's absolutely stunning!"

When Mia looks in the mirror, her face never gives away what she's thinking. She just scans herself like she's checking for cracks. Her dress is Hawaiian, white with huge bright blue hibiscus. It clings like sandwich wrap. Mom's right—it's a knockout.

The General is flustered, not her usual self at all. She flits around, offering hair spray, her favorite perfume. "How about just a little more eye shadow, Megan? It'll bring out the blue in your eyes." I wobble on my silver sandals over to her dresser and peer into the mirror. My eyes look okay to me. "You look lovely, Elaine," the General says. "Your hair's grown out so well!" Against the dark green taffeta of her dress, Elaine's face is ghostly pale. I know she's nervous. I would be, too, if my prom date was a complete stranger. She barely got a glimpse before Danny whisked him off to play basketball. Now they're in Danny's room. His name is Sal; he's a friend of Danny's and a Berkeley pre-law freshman. That's all we know for sure. Elaine says he's Italian. I can't tell how she feels about that.

My dress has see-through sleeves and shoulders. At Agatha's Attic, the General fell right in love with it, but she isn't the one who has to wear the strapless bra. I hike it up, pull it down. No way is it going to sit the way it's supposed to. I frown into the mirror. This isn't Megan. It's some Megan impostor transformed by aliens. It won't fool Joe for a minute.

"Okay, now, girls!" orders the General in her General's voice. "Time for pictures!" She lines us up, Mia the tallest in the middle, Elaine and I like bookends on either side. "Smile!" The ancient Polaroid snaps and buzzes and whirs. Out pops our first prom picture. "Oh!" the General cries, all fluttery again. "You look so grown up!"

We gather around to check ourselves out.

"What's wrong with this picture?" Mia says, but she already knows and so do we. We've tried not to mention the prom around Kit, but Elaine's been so nervous about it, she slipped a couple of times. Kit acted like she wasn't at all interested, but I could tell that she was. I knew she was thinking that if things had been different, she'd be shopping for a prom dress, too. Or at least borrowing something from Mia. She'd be in the picture, where we always thought she'd be.

"You ready up there?" Danny hollers up the stairs.

Elaine clutches my hand. I think she's going to faint. Even Mia looks a little shaky. "Hey, you guys, lighten up!" I say. "This is our prom, not a funeral!"

"Not *your* funeral," Mia says, giving herself a last once-over in the General's mirror.

"Remember what you said!" hisses Elaine as we totter down the stairs in our heels. "You won't leave me alone with this . . . with this Sal guy, right? You promised!"

My heart does a tumble when the boys turn, all three at once. But it's Joe's eyes I'm checking out, and suddenly I know what all this is for. It's for that glazed-over look Joe's got on his silly face. It's for power.

Even Dad's at a loss for words. "Well!" he says. "Well, well!"

We sort of clump there in the hallway, nobody knowing what to do or say next. Then everybody starts talking at once. "You girls look great!" says Danny. "Will it be warm enough, girls?" says the General. "Will you need jackets?" "Wait!" says Dad, "I'll get the good camera!" More pictures. This time, boy-girl, boy-girl. We're captured for all eternity there in the entryway of 1637 Sycamore. By the time we leave for the prom, everybody smells like the General's perfume, even the guys.

Taylor feels transformed. The prison-red bricks look softer, a muted pink. Windows gaze benevolently down as if to say, Who are you? Kids I see every day in English or Bio have changed overnight from worms to butterflies. Guys in slick white tuxedos reach for the hands of gorgeous grown-up women and lift them from long white limousines. I float alongside Joe—Megan the troublemaker, Megan the big mouth, Megan the suspended, Megan the transformed.

We dance to good songs played by a bad band, but even sour notes don't scatter the fairy dust. The gym is a place I've never been, that nobody's ever been before. It sparkles with a thousand mirrored lights. It hums with the gentle laughter of kids playing grown-ups, or maybe the laughter of kids who *are* grown-ups, at least for a few hours.

Mia swirls past, a blue-and-white vision in my brother's arms. Their eyes say nobody else is there, anywhere, for miles around. Elaine is laughing, batting her eyes at Sal, or maybe just blinking up at him through her seldom-worn contact lenses. I close my eyes and drift with Joe toward our own private island. It feels like years since we've all just had a plain old good time.

"Have fun," the General said as we left the house. She kissed me on the cheek, then wiped off the lipstick, quickly, with the heel of her hand. "Have the time of your life!" There were tears in her eyes.